The Legend of
Lovea Duval

The Legend of Lovea Duval

Mike Shepherd

THE LEGEND OF LOVEA DUVAL

This is a work of fiction. All of the characters, names, incidents, organizations, and dialogue in this novel are either the products of the author's imagination or are used fictitiously.

iUniverse books may be ordered through booksellers or by contacting:

iUniverse
1663 Liberty Drive
Bloomington, IN 47403
www.iuniverse.com
844-349-9409

Because of the dynamic nature of the Internet, any web addresses or links contained in this book may have changed since publication and may no longer be valid. The views expressed in this work are solely those of the author and do not necessarily reflect the views of the publisher, and the publisher hereby disclaims any responsibility for them.

Any people depicted in stock imagery provided by Getty Images are models, and such images are being used for illustrative purposes only. Certain stock imagery © Getty Images.

ISBN: 978-1-4502-0056-1 (sc)
ISBN: 978-1-4502-0057-8 (e)

Print information available on the last page.

iUniverse rev. date: 08/17/2023

Dedicated to
Jane

PART I

Chapter 1

Life was good for Mick Scott, living in the stone house he built at Lake Wells, deep in southern Illinois near Carbondale.

He had written a well-received book about his experiences as a correspondent for Armed Forces Radio in Vietnam, which provided enough money for him to live on without having to work a regular job. And the land the house sat on had been bought with the substantial amount of money he was paid by the CIA to infiltrate a faction of the Weather Underground in Carbondale in the late '60s and early '70s when the anti-war movement was extremely active there.

He had become acquainted with the CIA while doing research for his book at the controversial Vietnamese Studies Center at Southern Illinois University. The Center had been infiltrated (it was thought by its director David Gordon) by the Weather Underground, who wanted to expose it for being affiliated with the CIA. Consequently Gordon wanted to infiltrate them to verify his suspicion that they had infiltrated the Center. Gordon recruited Scott to do the job.

Because of his experience in infiltrating the Weather Underground, and as a correspondent for Armed Forces Radio, the CIA was interested in recruiting him for a new assignment. They needed someone to serve as a correspondent for Voice of America to secretly report on Communist atrocities in Cambodia.

Gordon was sent to Lake Wells to personally recruit Scott for the Cambodian job.

"I had a hunch our paths would cross again someday, Mick," David said as they shook hands at the front door of Scott's house.

David had changed some since the last time they saw each other. He had a bit of a belly now, that his 6 foot 4 inch frame appeared to minimize, and a receding hairline. He still smoked a pipe, which he lit after they shook hands.

"Come in, Man, it's good to see you again. To what do I owe the honor of this visit?"

"I'll get right to the point."

"Well sit down first, here at the table. Coffee? I don't have any booze."

"Sure."

"How do you like it?"

"Black will be fine."

"Comin' right up." Mick sat down at the table with two cups of coffee. "You were saying."

As was his old habit, David took a drag from the pipe, put his head back and puffed a couple of smoke rings into the air, then he spoke.

"Well, Mick, as was expected and feared, once the U.S. withdrew from South Vietnam, all of Southeast Asia fell to the Communists. The Domino Theory has come to pass. They've taken over Laos, and two weeks after the fall of Saigon the Khmer Rouge, led by Pol Pot, conquered Cambodia. He immediately declared 1975 as Year Zero and he ordered city dwellers, particularly those in Phnom Penh, the capital, to be evacuated to labor camps in the countryside to fulfill his quest for an agrarian utopia. This caused the displacement of more than three million people. Thousands who failed to cooperate have been killed, along with anyone with ties to the French. Many more who were educated -- teachers, doctors, lawyers and business men and women -- have been executed simply because they were considered to be Capitalist and too bourgeois. At the present pace the death toll is expected to reach millions. We need someone to go there and report this to the world through Voice of America. You're our prime candidate, Mick."

"Voice of America in Cambodia? How in the hell would I pull that off?"

"You'd be posing as a correspondent for Radio Moscow, which would entail learning some Russian. While Pol Pot has ordered the expulsion of Soviet diplomats, he's allowing a select few Soviet journalists to stay in country who will put a positive spin on the revolution, to enhance

Cambodia's status in the eyes of the rest of the Communist world, which to me would be difficult, considering how bloody it is. We'd make it well worth your while financially. Yes, it would be dangerous, but you're no stranger to that. What a ya say?"

Mick thought about it for a moment while David puffed on his pipe.

"When would I leave?"

"For Cambodia, in a year, meanwhile we'd send you to Washington to learn a little Russian at CIA headquarters, then we'll instruct you about how to enter Cambodia and what to do once you're there."

"How long would the assignment last?"

"Including your time in Washington, about two years."

As a Vietnam veteran frustrated by the way the war had ended -- with a Communist takeover of all of the old Indochina -- Mick saw the assignment as an opportunity to have some impact on how the rest of the world viewed Communism. Communists professed to be for the common man -- the proletariat -- but in the process (going back to Stalin and Mao), they murdered millions who would not march in lockstep with them. Pol Pot was doing the same in Cambodia, apparently, and the world needed to be told about it through Voice of America.

"Okay, I'll go."

"Great, Mick, I knew you would." David smiled. "You'll have to leave Monday; that gives you three days. Meanwhile I'll arrange for you to fly from Carbondale to St. Louis, where you'll catch a flight to D.C. When you get there, take a cab to CIA headquarters. Your contact there will be Jason Wade. He'll set you up in a hotel and give you the schedule for your Russian language course."

"What about money?"

"You'll be given plenty for expenses up front, and when you've completed the course and are ready to depart for Cambodia, you'll be paid $20,000 for the assignment, which will be deposited in your bank here in Carbondale. You'll be given $5,000 in Russian rubles and U.S. dollars to be used on the assignment. The Cambodian riel has been abolished by Pol Pot and the Khmer Rouge, but they're not adverse to having a few greenbacks floating around, especially if those end up in their pockets. Keep your dollars in reserve, though, they could come in handy in a pinch. Also, upon the completion of the course, Wade will fill you in on all the details of how you'll get to Cambodia and where you'll stay while in Phnom Penh.

"Okay, that's it, Mick, on this end. I better go before it gets too dark, I don't like walking in the woods when it's dark. Your flight leaves Carbondale for St. Louis at 9 a.m. Monday. Good luck."

David gave Mick a hardy handshake and left.

It would be difficult for Mick to leave Kathy, his girlfriend of two years, and Carmella the dog, and Jazzpur the cat. When he told Kathy about the assignment, she expressed how fearful she was for him, but she agreed to live in his house and take care of the pets in his absence.

Chapter 2

Mick had never been to Washington D.C. It was a good time to be there: July 1976, the 200th anniversary of the nation's birth. The entire city was decorated with bunting, banners and flags, as he saw on his cab ride from Dulles Airport to CIA headquarters, a grey stone, nondescript monolithic-like building, as the Agency liked to keep a low profile. But the spacious lobby was more conspicuous with the CIA's symbol inlaid on the shiny marble floor.

At the front desk Mick told the receptionist he was to meet with a Jason Wade. She directed him to Wade's office on the third floor.

He was a stocky man, but he appeared to be fit. His hair was cut short, military-style. He introduced himself with a slight smile and a quick handshake, then he got straight to the point.

"David Gordon told me all about you. Infiltrated the Weather Underground. Dangerous group. Now you'll be messing with the Khmer Rouge, even more dangerous. They're cold-blooded killers. You'll learn a little about them and their leader Pol Pot in these classes you're taking. The primary focus will be, as you know, learning Russian well enough to get by among Cambodians. And you'll learn a little Cambodian too. We're putting you up in a Sheraton Hotel a few blocks from here. Take cabs, get receipts, we'll reimburse you. And here's a credit card for meals and such. All expenses will be charged to the CIA."

Mick attended classes from nine to three each day. At night in his room he went over what he had learned that day, of the Russian and Cambodian languages, and Cambodian history, primarily as it involved the Khmer Rouge and Pol Pot.

Khmer Rouge translated "Red Cambodians," and was the term describing the Communist party in Kampuchea, as it is now called by the Communists, instead of Cambodia. They are led by Pol Pot, who, as a teenager in the 1940's, left his peasant upbringing and joined the forces of Ho Chi Minh to fight both the Japanese and the French. He became secretary of the Cambodian Communist party in 1963. During that same year he retreated into the Cambodian jungles, and, with assistance from the Vietnamese Communists, formed the Khmer Rouge guerrillas. They opposed the neutral government of Prince Sihanouk, who supported the secret American bombing and invasion of Cambodia in 1969 and 1970. And when General Lon Nol, an American sympathizer, deposed Sihanouk, the Khmer Rouge, led by Pol Pot, strengthened its position in Cambodia, isolating Lon Nol's army within city fortresses and forcing their surrender in 1975.

After a month of attending classes and studying in his room, Mick got bored with the routine and ventured out into Washington, to a bar not far from the hotel. Feeling very Russian, he ordered a vodka and tonic. He hadn't drunk in months, and the first one made his head swim, so he left the bar and walked around for a while, eventually arriving at the Mall. He looked up and was taken aback by the simple splendor of the Washington Monument. He hadn't realized it was so broad-based and tall. There were no skyscrapers in D.C., symbols of America's great commercial wealth, only monuments, symbols of our great heritage. Walking around, Mick was surprised that there was no monument honoring Eisenhower, the man who led the Allies in WWII, and no memorial to WWII itself, the country's greatest war. And, of course, there would never be a memorial to the Vietnam War, the saddest war, in which more than 50,000 American men died fighting for the freedom of another people, only for the war to end before the job was finished. Some say the U.S. lost the war, but we only lost the resolve to help the South Vietnamese win it. Thinking of it all made Mick sad, so on the way back to the hotel he stopped at the bar again, and drank until last call.

Learning Russian with a hangover wasn't so hard, after all the Russians spoke it all the time with hangovers from drinking too much vodka. Mick had them stereotyped. He pictured haggard women in drab house dresses with their hair done up in scarves, standing in line at the meat market for ham bones for a paltry cabbage soup, prepared in the small kitchen of a cramped high rise apartment, where entire families lived in a space only big enough for two.

The Soviets were poor. Communism wasn't working so well for them, especially regarding agriculture. That's why they had to buy so much grain and meat from the U.S. to feed their people So why would Radio Moscow, Mick asked his Russian language instructor, want to propagandize Communism's attempt at an agrarian utopia in Cambodia, of all places, when it seemed to be failing in the USSR?

"Because they are holding out hope that one day Communism will dominate the world by uniting the proletariat in developing countries like those in Southeast Asia and in Red China, Cuba and North Korea, for example," the instructor said, "while the Soviet Union, through a series of five-year plans, strives to become a Marxist/Leninist utopia that will rule the Communist world. To their credit, they are forever optimistic, despite the failures."

Chapter 3

Occasionally Mick went to the bar that he'd discovered, down the street from his hotel. He liked it because of its unique mix of clientele: old and young and men and women, and long hairs, and guys with GI haircuts. Walter Reed Army Hospital wasn't too far away. One particular guy who came in every Saturday night on crutches was a patient there. He had a way of sneaking out of the hospital with the assistance of a nurse, he told Mick after they became acquainted.

"I lost my leg, Man, but I haven't lost my taste for rum," he said in a gravelly voice with an Hispanic accent.

He was one of the long hairs; locks black and shiny as coal, kept in check with a red bandanna. His eyes and his skin were dark. His name was Pedro. Mick learned that he was Puerto Rican. Because Puerto Rico was a territory of the U.S., he'd been drafted into the U.S. Army, and lost his leg in Vietnam. But he had no regrets, "Except I can't do the rumba anymore."

Mick had enough drinks to ask him how he lost his leg.

"I was walking point on the last patrol by American forces in Vietnam. We were trying to secure a road for refugees fleeing the fighting just outside Saigon, and I fricking stepped into a camouflaged pit and ran a fricking punji stake up through my foot. They'd dipped 'em in dung. I got an infection. They tried for months to save my leg but gangrene set in and they had to amputate, Man. I've been rehabbing at the hospital ever since, but I'm due to be discharged soon."

One night Pedro came in with a woman he introduced as Susan, his nurse. "She helps me sneak out of the hospital on Saturday nights," Pedro said. She shushed him.

Susan had short blond hair and blue eyes. When she sat next to Pedro, they looked like people from two different worlds. They were: she was from Minnesota, and of Swedish descent.

The war had brought many people from many different backgrounds together. Mick and a Vietnamese woman named Tron, the daughter of a Saigon baker, had come together by happenstance, and had almost married, but she and her family went to Hong Kong in exile after the bakery was bombed by the Viet Cong, because her father, a former Communist and confidant of Ho Chi Minh had become a Capitalist.

That was a long time ago -- eight years since Mick had been in Vietnam. It had been only a little more than a year, though, for Pedro. He had seen Saigon fall, just two weeks after Phnom Penh went down. A few months later the Communist Pathet Lao conquered Laos. The dominos had fallen all right, as they were expected to, once the U.S. withdrew its forces from Southeast Asia, and a bloodbath had begun in Cambodia.

"If I could grow another fricking leg, Man, I'd go back as a mercenary," Pedro said, "and join up with an anti-Communist counterinsurgency."

"There is one?" Mick asked.

"I don't know, Man, but there should be, we've got a lot of unfinished business to tend to over there."

"No, it's finished, Pedro," Susan said. "The Communists won, accept it."

"Yeah, but it's a bitter pill to swallow," Pedro said with resignation while shaking his head and staring at his rum and Coke. Susan rubbed his shoulder.

"It's time for you guys to come home," she said, knowing that Mick was a Vietnam vet too.

"Salute', Pedro," Mick said, and they clanked glasses and drank, and drank. Every Saturday night for a month they met at the same bar, but then Susan and Pedro stopped coming. Another month went by and Susan showed up, in tears.

"Mick, Pedro died of a staph infection last week. We were going to be married at Christmas, y'know. He planned to have you as his best man. I'm going to try to get him buried in Arlington National

Cemetery. He was highly decorated. He won the Distinguished Service Cross, the nation's second highest award for valor in combat, and the Purple Heart, of course. He deserves a special place of honor, don't you think?"

"Yes I do. Contact me at my hotel when you find out if it can be done."

Two days later Mick got a message that Pedro would indeed be buried at Arlington.

The hardest part for Mick was when they played the Taps. As with the Irish ballad *Danny Boy*, every time he heard it he cried inside.

Chapter 4

By the time spring came to Washington and the cherry blossoms bloomed Mick had learned enough Russian to get by. To test him, Wade took him to a restaurant near the Soviet Embassy where their diplomats drank and dined. The waiter spoke Russian and Jason carried on a superficial conversation with him, inviting Mick to join in. Mick passed the test.

After dinner, over a vodka or two, Wade filled Mick in on the logistics of his assignment.

"Tomorrow it's on to the CIA office in L.A. where you'll collect your fake Soviet credentials. You'll then fly to Singapore. From there to Rangoon where you'll hook up with Ross Monroe at the Voice of America studio. Someone at the airport, or a cabby, should know where it is. Monroe will instruct you further, and provide you with a tape recorder and tapes. Here are your airline tickets and two thousand dollars in greenbacks for expenses. Keep a couple hundred hidden. You won't be spending much. There's not much left in Phnom Penh to spend anything on.

"Okay, that's it, Scott. Your payment for the assignment has been deposited in your Carbondale bank. Good luck. If there's any indication that they're on to you, get the hell out of there on the plane that goes back and forth between Rangoon and Phnom Penh."

Wade left Mick alone at the restaurant, where he continued practicing Russian ordering vodkas and engaging in small talk with the waiter. In the morning, with a rip-roaring hangover, he flew to Los Angeles, went to the CIA office to collect his credentials then returned to the airport for his flight to Singapore. From there he caught a plane to Rangoon. All in all from Washington to Rangoon he had been in the air for about 36 hours. Having traversed several time zones and climates, when he finally disembarked at mid-day in the hot and steamy Burmese capital his head swam from jet lag. To pep him up, he needed a drink before doing anything else; a cold one, a beer. He went straight to the airport bar and was surprised to see that they served his favorite, Budweiser. He had one while watching people walk by -- mostly men in Nehru jackets, slacks and sandals with pillbox-like hats. The few women who were there wore long, colorful, silky dresses and matching scarves on their heads – arms, hands and necks adorned with an abundance of golden jewelry, reflecting the wealth of those who could afford to fly, instead of taking the crowded trains over Burma's rugged terrain.

No one seemed to be in much of a hurry like they were in L.A., walking around at about the same pace as the ceiling fans that spun lazily above, stirring the hot air. Mick decided that he wasn't in that much of a hurry either since Voice of America was expecting him anytime within the next day or so, so he had another beer, then he sauntered over to the information desk to find out where Voice of America was, if anyone knew. The woman at the desk didn't, but she suggested Mick ask a cabby.

"Okay, yes, take you there," the first cabby he hailed said.

Speeding down the busy, broad streets of downtown Rangoon, Mick caught glimpses of the city's architecture, obviously influenced by both the East and the West – Oriental and primarily English as Burma had been a British colony dating back to the 1880s, before being occupied by the Japanese in WWII. After the war, in 1948, it gained its independence from Great Britain, but English had become Burma's widely-spoken second language, and the cabby knew it well -- well enough to know that Mick had an American accent.

"You will be on the radio?" he asked, "for Voice of America?"

Mick was hesitant to answer the question, but what harm could there be in revealing as much to an ordinary cab driver?

"Yes," Mick said.

"Very good," the cabby said gleefully, glancing at Mick through the rear view mirror. "I listen to it often. Gives good news about what is going on in the free world compared to what we hear from radio in China and Vietnam about the Communist world," he said.

Apparently he was not an ordinary cabby after all, but one who was politically aware.

"Are the Communists active in Burma?" Mick asked.

"Only far away from the city."

"That's how they started in Vietnam and Cambodia," Mick replied.

"Yes, I know. That's why Voice of America is so important, to keep track of what they are up to."

They no longer traveled on broad boulevards, but on narrow side streets on the outskirts of the capital. Suddenly they were forced to stop as a line of elephants guided by a man with a stick, passed in front of them. The cabby laughed at Mick's look of astonishment.

"They are used in that teakwood sawmill just up the block. The logs are very heavy, only elephants can handle."

After another mile or so of driving on side streets, they came to a wider one called Mandalay Road which led away from Rangoon to the north, and the cabby pulled over and pointed to an inconspicuous house -- a cottage to be more exact, with shuttered windows – with a large white satellite dish on the roof. In the front yard, hanging on a light post, was a small wooden sign that simply said, "Voice of America."

"This is it," the cabby said.

Mick paid the fare and tipped him well in greenbacks since he had none of the Burmese currency kyats. Jason Wade had said dollars would sometimes come in handy.

Mick tried the front door. It opened. He poked his head in and called out, "Hello?"

At first no one answered. "Hello," he said again. This time a man appeared from a back room.

"Hello," he responded. "Can I help you?"

"I'm Mick Scott."

"Oh, yeah, Mick, great to meet you, I'm Ross Monroe."

They shook hands.

Monroe looked more like a disc jockey than a newsman, with his hip-hugging bell bottom jeans, wide belt and a paisley brown, orange and green shark-fin collared shirt. He had fairly long hair (reddish in color like Mick's), muttonchops and a mustache -- looking very '70s.

"Mick, it's great to put a face to a name. I recall hearing a couple of your reports from Armed Forces Radio, Vietnam. They fed us material. When was it now, must have been five or six years ago. I was stationed in West Berlin."

"It would have been about eight years, actually," Mick said.

"That's right, the report was on the Tet Offensive of '68. Wow, time marches on. Well, let's go back to the studio."

They left the front room which also served as an office, and they stepped into the studio. It reminded Mick of the one in which he worked in Saigon. It had acoustical tile on the walls and ceiling, and a master control board with a microphone and various tape recorders: an 8-track, a cassette and a reel-to-reel recorder.

"Coffee?" Monroe asked.

"Sure, I could use a cup."

"Welcome to Burma," Monroe said, touching his cup to Mick's.

"We're keeping a low profile here, with the exception of the rather conspicuous dish on the roof. The neutralist government of Ne Win is cordial to Voice of America because they are concerned about the recent fall of South Vietnam, Cambodia and Laos to the Communists. Burmese Communist insurgents are very active on the northeastern frontier bordering Laos, and in the southeast along the border with Thailand. There have been battles with the government forces and many have been killed.

"Ne Win recently took delivery of several U.S. helicopters, ostensibly to combat opium smuggling in these regions, but there is speculation that the choppers will be used to combat the Communists. Also Washington has been approached about the procurement of other weapons to be used against the rebels, so Ne Win is hardly neutral in this respect."

Monroe went on to say that Pol Pot was presently isolated and seeking an ally in the region because he was at odds with Vietnam, and so he was open to diplomatic relations with Burma and thus allowed flights in and out of Rangoon and Phnom Penh as he kisses up to Ne

Win in hopes of persuading him to give the Burmese Communists a voice in his government.

"You'll be able to get your reports to us on these flights," Monroe said. "The pilot, Lam Linh, and his co-pilot, Tran Van are thought by the Khmer Rouge to be Vietnamese Communist, like the many who joined the fight against Lon Nol's government troops. They thought the two had flown in the North Vietnamese Air Force, but in reality, they secretly flew for the CIA's Air America in South Vietnam. When the North Vietnamese Army was about to surround Saigon in 1975, while still working for the CIA, they painted their DC-3 with North Vietnamese Air Force insignias and flew into Cambodia pretending to be couriers for the Khmer Rouge from outposts into Phnom Penh. This gave them access to battle plans that they relayed by radio to CIA listening posts in neighboring Thailand.

"When the Khmer Rouge captured the Cambodian capital they were assigned by Pol Pot himself to fly supplies in, primarily food, twice weekly from Rangoon and Bangkok, for the privileged politburo. In the process they passed on what secrets they learned to the CIA offices in those cities.

"Also they'll be passing your tapes on to me, after they've been given to them by Pich Sabay, your contact in Phnom Penh. Sabay will appear to be close friends of Lam Linh and Tran Van as they mingle and shake hands at the airport by the plane before departing for Rangoon. That's when your tapes will be stealthily passed on to them. Sabay is also thought by the Khmer Rouge to be a Communist. He is, in deed, a former Communist who now poses as an official with Pol Pot's Ministry of Information."

"How will I make contact with him?" Mick inquired.

"Your meeting with him has been pre-arranged. He's expecting you on tonight's flight to Phnom Penh. It arrives early in the morning. He'll be waiting for you at customs to serve as your escort when you go to the countryside to do stories for Radio Moscow, at least so the Khmer Rouge think. The two of you will then make arrangements in private about how you'll put the tapes in his hands, so that he in turn can get them to Lam Linh, who I'll meet at the Rangoon airport every Wednesday and Sunday night to get the tapes.

"Follow me, Mick? I know it sounds a little complicated, but if everyone does their part it'll work out fine. Basically it's pretty simple. You'll be giving the tapes to Sabay, he in turn will pass them on to Lam Linh who will give them to me at the airport in Rangoon."

"I follow you."

Chapter 5

Phnom Penh's airport was mostly deserted, except for a few soldiers milling about, and a stern-looking man sitting at a desk at customs who asked to see Mick's visa. He looked it over with one eyebrow raised, as if suspicious of its validity, and of the tape recorder Mick carried. He then asked Mick many questions in broken Russian about the exact nature of his visit.

"Why is Radio Moscow so interested in our affairs?"

"Because of your agricultural revolution. It is at the heart of original Russian Communism when the peasantry ruled the land sharing equally in what was produced by their strong lean hands. It will be a model for developing countries like Kampuchea to follow."

The man looked impressed.

"You are very fortunate to be here. Most all other Soviets have been expelled, but Pol Pot has personally allowed your presence," he said, "but you will not venture into the countryside without soldiers, and your reports will be closely monitored. You will stay at the Hotel Angkor on Mekong Boulevard. Before you leave every day for the countryside, you will be escorted, along with the soldiers, by this man Pich Sabay who works with the Ministry of Information."

There was a man standing off to one side who nodded at Mick when customs pointed him out. He was a middle-aged man who was relatively tall for a Cambodian, and very thin. He wore a black shirt and black slacks. He stood with his hands behind him, waiting patiently to be introduced.

"Any questions?"

"Yes, is there a restaurant in the hotel? I'm very hungry."

"No restaurant anymore. You may go now. He will take you to the hotel," the man at customs nodded toward Pich Sabay, who walked with Mick to the front door of the airport. Soldiers standing nearby gave Mick the once over and they said something about him that made them laugh as he passed. It wasn't a joyful laugh, but one of ridicule.

"They don't like foreigners," Sabay said in Russian.

"Yes, I can tell," Mick responded in Russian.

Sabay led the way to his car, a French Renault which was familiar to Mick, as they were used as taxis in Saigon. In the privacy of his car, Sabay opened up in English.

"You know of my role in this scheme, I assume. You will pass the tapes on to me at midnight on the day you record them for Voice of America, at the hotel, in your room. The soldiers are never there that late. I, in turn, will get them to the pilots at the airport on the morning the flights depart for Rangoon, while shaking their hands at the plane, as we pretend to be close friends, comrades-in-arms so to speak -- at least so it will appear to the soldiers should they be watching. However, neither of us are comrades in the Communist sense, although at one time I truly was a Communist."

Sabay, who had a marked nervous twitch of his left eye that made him look like he was constantly winking, went on to explain how things had changed. He, like Pol Pot left his peasant background as a teenager in the 1940's and joined the forces of Ho Chi Minh in battling both the Japanese, who occupied Indochina during WWII, and then the French, who occupied Indochina as colonists before WWII. When Indochina was divided into Cambodia, Laos and South and North Vietnam by the Geneva Conference of 1954, following the French defeat at Dien Binh Phu at the hands of Ho Chi Minh (General Giap to be more exact).

"Prince Sihanouk ruled Cambodia and he tried to maintain neutrality between the U.S. and Communist powers, including North Vietnam," Sabay said. "However, Pol Pot, who had become a leader in the Cambodian Communist Party opposed Sihanouk's less-than-neutral alliance with the West, so he, along with the Khmer Rouge, waged guerrilla warfare against the Prince." Sabay, being a Communist, joined the Khmer Rouge and became a lieutenant.

When Sihanouk went to France in 1970 he entrusted the country to Prime Minister Lon Nol, who, being vehemently anti-Communist and tired of Sihanouk's neutrality in the Indochina conflict, engineered a coup in which the National Assembly ousted the Prince and placed Lon Nol in complete power. As a result, the Khmer Rouge stepped up their guerrilla warfare against Lon Nol's forces, and by 1971 they controlled most of the country. In 1975, when they conquered the capital, Phnom Penh, Sabay, because of his experience in the field producing leaflets that were distributed to villages promoting the Communist cause, was appointed to the Ministry of Information, a propagandist arm of Pol Pot's regime. But, Sabay said, he privately opposed the murderous ways of the new dictator and he went over to the CIA, which had Asian moles operating in Cambodia right under the nose of the Khmer Rouge in an effort to undermine Pol Pot by instigating dissent among the ranks of the upper echelon in the politburo, thereby capitalizing on their extreme paranoia which is inherent among revolutionaries.

"They were always looking over their shoulders expecting some bold underling to attempt a coup. I have often thought of organizing one myself, but at the present time, while working for the Ministry of Information I will be content with smuggling your reports on the atrocities of the Khmer Rouge to Voice of America in Rangoon under the auspices of the CIA."

Sabay's eye twitched repeatedly. He seemed quite nervous, and understandably so, scheming the way he was right under Pol Pot's nose.

"So there you have it, Mick Scott. This is where I am now."

As they drove along to the hotel, Mick could see the telltale signs of the battles that had occurred between Lon Nol's government troops and the Khmer Rouge: bullet-riddled buildings, rubble and burned-up vehicles everywhere. And there were still corpses lying about, rotting and covered with flies. Finally they came to a wide boulevard lined with stately French-style buildings, some with gated walls in front. They looked deserted, as did the entire city of Phnom Penh, with the exception of the ubiquitous soldiers who patrolled the streets in Jeeps. Sabay pulled up to a multi-storied building with ornate iron balconies and a pillared facade. A tarnished brass placard on one of the pink marble pillars said "Hotel Angkor" in English. Strange, Mick thought, this was an old French colonial city, but English was the international language of travel. Even in Paris some of the hotel signs were in English he had learned on a trip he had taken there when he first got out of the service.

"You will stay in room 202," Sabay said as they entered the hotel. "But the room must remain unlocked at all times. So much for privacy under this regime," he said in a low tone, looking over his shoulder. "When you record your reports for Voice of America you'll need to watch very closely who might be listening at your door. They are very suspicious of foreigners, even though they think you are a Communist, too."

They paused momentarily in the lobby which was situated amid four pink and gray marble Corinthian columns that rose to a ceiling domed with yellow leaded glass glowing from sunlight, forming a rotunda of sorts. The leaves of the long-neglected potted tropical plants had turned brown; some of their leaves had fallen and littered the marble floor.

"It appears that the life has gone out of this hotel," Sabay said. "I am told it used to be a popular gathering place for foreigners, primarily French and Soviets."

Mick looked around. The periphery of the sunlit lobby was dark. The adjoining restaurant was closed – chairs and stools turned upside down on the tables and bar. It reminded Mick of how empty his stomach was.

Far off in the shadows he spotted a wide, winding staircase that was visible because of the footlights and the brass banister that reflected the light of the lobby.

"I'll walk you to your room," Sabay said, and they ascended the stairs to the second floor. A window at the end of the hall provided enough light to see the room numbers. 202 was at the top of the stairs. Sabay opened the door. "I'll leave you to settle in."

"I'm awfully hungry, Sabay. Where can I get some food?"

"If you can wait until tomorrow morning when I come I'll bring bananas and grapefruit. Fish is sometimes available on the waterfront but we've no place to cook it. You'd have to eat it raw."

"Uh, I think I'll hold off on that for a while."

"Very well, I'll return for you at seven o'clock in the morning and we will drive to the village of Kampong Luong where much rice is grown. You will see the abuse the workers endure. I'll be accompanied by soldiers in a jeep who will follow us. Remember to speak Russian in their presence. I'll leave you to rest now. Goodbye."

The room was nicely furnished, but it smelled musty. The bed clothes were stale and dusty, Mick discovered, when he fluffed the pillows before lying down. He lay awake for awhile, stomach growling from hunger, mind racing from having flown practically nonstop for several days, but he finally fell asleep.

When the sun shone through the window onto his face, he woke up. At first he didn't know where he was, until his head cleared and he remembered arriving in Phnom Penh and coming to the hotel with a man named Sabay. He looked at his watch, it was nearly seven o'clock. Sabay would be there soon. They'd be going to a place called Kampong Luong where much rice was being grown. They'd be escorted by Khmer Rouge soldiers who'd be listening closely to what he reported about what was going on there, ostensibly for Radio Moscow. He'd put a positive spin on it for their benefit of course, but that night in the hotel he'd record for Voice of America a report on the brutality the soldiers exercised to keep the workers in line.

Sabay arrived with bananas and grapefruits. Mick devoured some of each.

"The soldiers are waiting," Sabay said.

They went downstairs and out the front door of the hotel to Sabay's car, parked in front of a Jeep in which four scowling soldiers sat. Sabay drove away slowly. The soldiers followed closely. Outside the city the terrain quickly became rice paddies as far as the eye could see. Men and women in black clothes wearing conical hats, guarded by armed soldiers, were obviously being forced to work. Some of the soldiers, who were also dressed in black, stood in the shade of palms smoking, while the workers toiled in the sun and suffocating humidity, knee-deep in water.

"It can be very dangerous working in the rice paddies. There are cobras," Sabay said. "And if a soldier believes a worker is not keeping up, he may be shot dead on the spot. The Khmer Rouge are very impatient and very cruel," he said in the privacy of the car as they drove along. "They also shoot those who have ties to Lon Nol and the French. There are many open graves to prove it. The bodies are piled high. They don't bother to cover them. If we can get away from the soldiers one day I will show you at the city of Kampong Cham where mass executions have taken place. Meanwhile I will show you the encampment at Kampong Luong where the workers live in long houses -- men and women, husbands and wives separately."

They turned off of the highway and onto a dirt road that led into the village where a section of the long houses were located. Sabay stopped the car and he and Mick got out. The soldiers left their jeep and stood close to the two. Sabay and Mick spoke in Russian.

"Would you like to see inside the houses?" Sabay asked Mick.

"Yes."

Sabay told the soldiers in Cambodian what they were going to do.

"As you can see they are very austere -- just cots draped in mosquito nets. Small trunks for change of clothes, and books and notepad and pencil to study Communism. They must be re-educated to live in Cambodia now."

"Yes, very austere," Mick observed.

"Yes," Sabay said. "Some of these people used to live in villas in the cities. It is very difficult for them to adjust. Many who don't are executed."

Mick stepped aside and pretended to be recording a report for Radio Moscow. In Russian he said that Cambodians from all walks of life who had relocated to the countryside were happily growing rice to feed their countrymen, and to make Cambodia a leading exporter of the grain on the world market again, after five years of unproductivity under the corrupt regime of Lon Nol, when Cambodians virtually starved while the pro-Western, anti-Communist Lon Nol waged war against the Khmer Rouge, who have become the people's saviors.

Listening to Mick's diatribe in Russian, the soldiers grew bored and dispersed to the shade of a nearby stand of palms where they smoked hand-rolled cigarettes.

When Mick finished his fake report he and Sabay went to the car and waited for the workers to return from the paddies. It was near sundown – they'd be coming soon.

The soldiers continued to linger in the shade, seemingly uninterested in Sabay and Mick. After a while the workers appeared in the distance walking in a straight line on the high ground between paddies, accompanied by soldiers. Suddenly the procession stopped and one of the soldiers yanked a worker from the line, forced him to his knees, put the barrel of his rifle to his head and shot. The worker fell face down and they dragged him off, and the procession continued on to the long houses.

"Why did he shoot him, Sabay?"

"Probably hadn't been cooperating. There is no room for rebellion here."

The soldiers who had accompanied Mick and Sabay to the village came over to the car.

"Go now," they ordered. "Go now back to Phnom Penh."

Sabay drove away and the soldiers again followed closely behind them.

When they arrived it was dark in the capital, except at the entrance of the hotel, which was faintly lit by an ornate light fixture above the door. Sabay dropped Mick off.

"I will be back at 1 a.m. for the tape. The soldiers are not around the hotel past midnight. You witnessed something today that would be of great interest to Voice of America, I'm sure."

Mick went up to his room and recorded an authentic report for Voice of America.

The people of Phnom Penh, city dwellers from all walks of life, have been forced to labor in Cambodia's steamy, cobra-infested rice paddies like those of Kampong Luong where they live in long houses and sleep on moldy cots. They work from sunup to sundown subsisting on two meager bowls of rice a day. They are expected to work hard; if not, they could be shot on the spot, as I witnessed today.

From deep inside Cambodia, where the Khmer Rouge rule with a bloody iron hand, this is Mick Scott reporting.

At 1 a.m. he went downstairs to meet Sabay. Mick slipped him the tape and Sabay left quickly. On his way back upstairs Mick caught a glimpse of a fleeting shadow in the closed restaurant. Was it a soldier watching Sabay and Mick? If so, why would he not want to be seen. The Khmer Rouge had no compunction about confronting anyone who acted suspiciously, especially a foreigner and a civilian. That's what Sabay was now, although he was closely connected to the Khmer Rouge as a member of the Ministry of Information, or propaganda, however one wished to characterize it.

Mick stood still for a while waiting to see if the shadow reappeared, and it did, ever-so-briefly. Someone was most definitely watching Mick. Curiosity got the better of him. He stepped over the rope and into the restaurant, and he saw a small figure running away into the kitchen. He followed far enough to see it disappear behind a cabinet that was seemingly flush against the wall, like a ghost vanishing. Was he hallucinating from hunger? Must have been. He returned to his room.

Chapter 6

Prey Lovea Duval's father Guy had been one of the French archaeologists involved in reclaiming the magnificent Angkor Wat shrines from the jungle where they had become overgrown after centuries of neglect.

Guy and his fellow archaeologists occasionally retreated to Phnom Penh for recreation and relaxation. They stayed at the Hotel Angkor where Prey's mother Ney Youda, part owner of the hotel and a chef by trade, served as the manager of the restaurant. She and Guy met and eventually married, and Prey Lovea, who was named for her mother's native village, was born. Tragically Guy Duval died of malaria while working at Angkor Wat and Ney Youda Duval was left to raise Prey Lovea on her own. Over the years, other members of the expedition befriended Ney and her daughter, and when they were in Phnom Penh, there were good times at the restaurant and bar where the wine flowed freely. Here Prey Lovea learned from the Frenchmen of the vintages. One Frenchman in particular, a dashing young man named Marcel, paid particular attention to her. She had graduated from a highly-regarded private school in the capital, but her mother convinced her to become the restaurant's maitre d' -- and an attractive maitre d' she made, having inherited her father's French good looks and height and the petite Cambodian beauty of her mother – a striking blend of Europe and Asia. Her long, silky black hair and gleaming hematite eyes and long legs made her stand out like a model. She wore Western clothes, as did her mother, as the restaurant catered to a primarily Western clientele.

Prey Lovea spoke French fluently, having learned it from her father at an early age. Many of the bourgeois of Cambodia spoke French, having been colonized by them for a hundred years. Marcel and Prey Lovea flirted in French, teasing each other to the amusement of the other men of the expedition. The others in turn teased the two for their adolescent flirtation. Eventually their relationship went far beyond merely flirting and they became engaged, but when the reclamation project at Angkor Wat concluded temporarily, Marcel was forced to return to France to work on another project there. They planned for Prey Lovea to join him in Paris in year or so, but those plans were continually put off, and she languished in Phnom Penh. Nearly two years passed, and in Marcel's last letter, he informed her that he was engaged to a French woman. Heartbroken, Prey Lovea eventually turned to another man to ease the pain -- an older Cambodian man named Long Samrong who frequented the restaurant and bar of the Hotel Angkor. He was a high-ranking official in Lon Nol's government. Prey escorted him to many state affairs, and she became known in governmental circles as a woman who, having been raised by an independent Westernized mother, wasn't afraid to express her political opinions among the men, which was unusual in the Cambodian culture of the day.

Samrong encouraged her to write a column for Phnom Penh's daily newspaper. He arranged a meeting for her up with the editorial board, and they were impressed with her ability to express her opinions in the samples of writings she submitted to them. She was decidedly anti-Communist, as the Khmer Rouge was emerging as a threat to the pro-West Lon Nol government under which entrepreneurship flourished. It was no secret that the Communists disdained free enterprise, the backbone of Capitalism. Being an entrepreneur, Prey Lovea saw this as a direct, personal threat (as an owner of the Hotel Angkor) and many enterprising Cambodians' way of life.

Her column appeared weekly under the by line Lovea (she dropped the Prey), and for months she denounced the Communists for their Marxist views, especially their desire to do away with all private property and to eliminate the middle class of which many Cambodia's entrepreneurs were members, including herself and her mother.

Lovea's anti-Communist columns were more than just the paranoid ranting of a Capitalist who feared the loss of her way of life. The threat the Khmer Rouge posed in Cambodia was all too real. They, along with their allies, the North Vietnamese Army, had, beginning in 1971, taken control of the countryside, and in 1974 they had pushed to within five miles of Phnom Penh, shelling the capital daily as they succeeded in capturing the former royal capital of Oudong, some 20 miles from Phnom Penh. Four months later Lon Nol's government forces recaptured Oudong from the Communist rebels, then, inexplicably Lon Nol made a significant departure from previous statements when he offered to negotiation peace with the Khmer Rouge without conditions. He had previously insisted on the withdrawal of all foreign troops (namely the North Vietnamese) from Cambodia, and the establishment of a cease-fire.

The rebels, confident of victory, rejected his overtures for peace, and they stepped up their war of insurgency while laying siege to Phnom Penh.

The constant, at-random shelling of the capital impacted its economy to the extent that many businesses were forced to close. But the Hotel Angkor continued to stay open, catering to many a brave soul who dared to venture out into the streets. The restaurant became a gathering place for many in Lon Nol's government who were planning what to do should the government fall to the Communists, which seemed inevitable. They would go into exile, and they tried to persuade Lovea and her mother to prepare to do the same. Lovea's older gentleman friend, Samrong, offered to take them with him.

"The airport is still open. We can fly to the Phillippines then on to Hawaii in the U.S.."

"No. The government troops will win out," Ney naively insisted, "and there will be peace and prosperity." Tears welled in her eyes. "Cambodia is my home. Prey Lovea is named for the village I was born in. We will stay."

But the shelling of Phnom Penh intensified as the Khmer Rouge surrounded the city, and many of Lon Nol's government, including Lon Nol himself, rushed to the airport and flew into exile to Hawaii.

Samrong went to the hotel and frantically urged Lovea and Ney to flee too.

"They are in the city now, and they are shooting people. They surely know of Lovea's writings. They will kill her!" Samrong said. But again Ney stubbornly refused.

"The Communist will take the hotel, Ney."

"If they do it will be over my dead body."

"Lovea, you come," Samrong pleaded.

"I must stay with my mother."

"Leave," Ney insisted.

"No, not without you."

"Very well then, we will go down to the wine cellar and hide there until the danger has passed. The government troops will oust the rebels like they did at Oudong."

"No, it is too late," Samrong said sadly. "I must go. Goodbye. Goodbye dear Lovea." And he dashed out the front door. As it opened the sound of shooting and explosions, that had been muffled before, rang out clearly. The enemy was close.

"Quickly, Lovea, come with me. We will get a mattress to take downstairs."

They took one from a room on the first floor, lugged it through the kitchen and pushed it down the stairs to the tunnel that led to the wine cellar.

"Clothes. We must have a change of clothes," Ney said. "Go upstairs to the suit and put some in a laundry bag, Lovea. Hurry! And we must have food."

Ney looked around. She spotted two full sacks of rice, dragged them to the cellar door and pushed them downstairs into the tunnel.

Lovea returned with the bag of clothes.

"Now fill that bucket with water and carry it down to the bottom of the stairs. Hurry, Prey Lovea, work hard. I'll get a hot plate and utensils. Oh, we must hide the door somehow. A curtain. No, better yet that cabinet. Help me push it in front of the door."

"But how will we pull it flush against the door from behind once we've gone into the stairs?" Lovea inquired.

Ney thought for a moment.

"Hooks. There are some with threads on them screwed into the wall holding utensils."

She removed two and screwed them into the back of the cabinet. They stepped down onto the stairs and pulled the cabinet by the hooks flush against the doorway, then they hauled all the necessities they had accumulated through the tunnel to the wine cellar.

For a week they cooked rice with some of the vegetables that had been stored in the cellar. The bucket of water they had taken down didn't last long; cooking with it and drinking some, and washing, so Ney was finally forced to go back up to the kitchen to get more. She had pushed the cabinet back up against the cellar door, but Lovea could hear the commotion anyway. She rushed to the top of the stairs and listened.

"Where is she? Where is this Lovea Duval, the anti-Communist writer? She was the maitre d' of this hotel, no?"

"No. I know not of whom you speak."

"You lie woman. On your knees!"

Then there was a gunshot. Lovea gasped.

"Mother, mother," she whispered, and she began to weep quietly. She soon got control of herself and continued to listen. It sounded like the soldiers were gone. There was deathly silence. She waited a little longer, then slowly pushed the cabinet away from the cellar door and stepped into the kitchen. There was a substantial pool of blood on the floor, looking as if her mother's body had been dragged through it, leaving a swath all the way out of the kitchen. Devastated, Lovea fell to her hands and knees and cried where her mother had been slain because she wouldn't tell the soldiers where her daughter was. There was nothing left to do but get another bucket of water and return to the cellar and continue to hide as the Khmer Rouge took control of Phnom Penh.

In the immediate aftermath of the fall of the capital, the new rulers of Cambodia, led by Pol Pot, ordered the evacuation of all the residents of the city and other urban centers into rural areas. More than 3 million urban dwellers (or the New People as they were being called), men, women, young and old, sick and well, rich and poor were forced to share in the rural experience of those who had been involved in the insurgency, and to begin the economic reconstruction of Cambodia on the basis of agricultural self-sufficiency, and the re-establishment of the country as a leading exporter of rice. In the process many did not survive because of the harsh conditions, the back-breaking work, the starvation and the brutality of the Khmer Rouge, punishing those who either failed to keep up or rebelled. Those with ties to the Lon Nol government or the French were being systematically executed. Lovea, a Lon Nol sympathizer and daughter of a Frenchman would surely meet that fate if they found her.

Chapter 7

The morning after Mick had been to Kampong Luong there was a knock on his door. It was Sabay.

"We can go now to Kampong Cham, without soldier escort. They won't know, they think I'm attending to other matters. Hurry please, I'll wait for you downstairs."

On the way to Kampong Cham Mick's mind drifted back to the night before when he saw someone in the kitchen of the hotel disappear behind a cabinet through the wall. He related what he thought he had seen to Sabay.

"Very curious," he said. "Could be Lovea Duval, the famous anti-Communist columnist who vanished when the Khmer Rouge conquered Phnom Penh. She was very outspoken against the Communist. They would surely kill her if they found her. She could be hiding in the hotel wine cellar."

Kampong Cham was about 50 miles up the Mekong River from Phnom Penh. The Mekong is widest and wildest in Cambodia after running along the border of Laos and Thailand from its source in Tibet. It surges 2,600 miles through China, Laos and the heart of Cambodia to its mouth on the South China Sea in Vietnam near Ho Chi Minh City, formerly Saigon, Sabay informed Mick.

Mick was no stranger to the Mekong River. He had been on it in Vietnam, well, at least on its shores -- in the city of Can Tho in a cellar bar called Sinbad's Galley where, as a reporter for Armed Forces Radio he was sent to interview a former U.S. Air Force commando (a Korean/American) who had been posing as a Viet Cong living in the infamous tunnels of Cu Chi. During the interview they got drunk and into a fight with three American sailors on R & R from a riverine outfit. The Shore Patrol was called to intervene. Mick wound up in the brig with a big black eye, a bloody lip that required stitches, and a missing front tooth. River towns are tough, Mick knew. He was born in one on the Mississippi, in Illinois. The Mekong reminded him of the Mississippi in a way. It was swift, wild, wide and muddy, but it was lined with palms instead of cottonwoods, and the boats plying the water were sampans and junks instead of ski boats, john boats and coal barges. But the sampans, flying Communist flags, were heavily-armed, Mick could see. Not even on the Mekong were Cambodians free.

They arrived in Kampong Cham mid-morning. The streets were deserted. This town, too had been abandoned, the citizenry having been relocated to so-called farms, but they were more like Stalin-era gulags, and as in Stalin's era, there were mass graves. With millions mass murdered there would be mass graves.

"It's in a field not far outside of the city," Sabay said. "It is basically an open grave. The Khmer Rouge didn't have the decency to completely cover the bodies with dirt."

Mick could smell it in the hot, humid, tropical air before they got there; the unmistakable stench of rotting flesh. Sabay stopped the car and they got out. From where Mick stood he saw the mass of fleshy bones and hairy skulls (some of which still had blindfolds wrapped around them) decomposing in the sun; a landscape so grotesque he fairly swooned from the sight of it. Flies buzzed around his face and he gagged.

"I've seen enough, Sabay. Let's go now before I vomit."

"Yes, it is difficult to digest, how Pol Pot and the Khmer Rouge could do this to so many of their own people. This is why I have turned against them. You must broadcast on Voice of America what you have seen here today, Mick. The world needs to know."

Back at the hotel Mick described on tape in words from a nightmare the mass grave at Kampong Cham, and he gave it to Sabay at one in the morning for him to take to the Vietnamese pilots at the airport to fly to Voice of America in Rangoon.

Later that morning there was a loud, hard knock on Mick's door. Before he could turn the knob to open it an angry-looking soldier barged in.

"Comrade So Lang wishes to see you at customs at the airport immediately."

"Is he the man who processed me in when I first arrived?"

"Probably so, he is the number one man in charge of customs. Come with me. Bring tape recorder and report you do for Radio Moscow, Comrade Lang said."

Another soldier waited out front in a Jeep. The three drove to the airport.

The last report Mick ostensibly did for Radio Moscow lauded the Khmer Rouge's efforts to ruralize Cambodian culture, apropos to one of Marx's and Engels's *Communist Manifesto* tenets regarding the gradual abolition of the distinction between town and country by relegating urban inhabitants to the countryside where they would work to restore Cambodia's position as a major exporter of rice and other agricultural products by establishing an agrarian utopia. This would undoubtedly impress Comrade Lang who was waiting with a scowl on his face for Mick.

"Play report for Radio Moscow," he ordered.

After listening to the tape there was a period of silence as So Lang folded his arms across his chest and glared at Mick.

"Why did you go to Kampong Cham without soldiers? What is to see there for Radio Moscow? You will not go anywhere anymore without soldiers. Understand? Pich Sabay will be told the same, and he will be disciplined for taking you to Kampong Cham alone. And you will have tape recorder taken away if there are any more indiscretions. Understood?"

"Yes, of course."

"Very well. Now go back to hotel and stay there until Sabay comes again with soldiers to take you to Takeo where rice is being grown at record rate. Radio Moscow will want to know. This is a model of labor efficiency. There is a school there also teaching the new way, to young and old alike. Everyone must learn the new way, beginning with Year Zero when we conquered Cambodia, now called Kampuchea."

The soldiers returned Mick to his hotel room, where he was to be confined until Sabay came to take him to Takeo.

By evening Mick grew very hungry. He hadn't eaten since early morning when he had bananas and grapefruit that Sabay brought along on their trip to Kampong Cham, but he dared not venture out beyond the hotel for food because Comrade So Lang had ordered him to stay put. Would there be any food in the kitchen? Something non-perishable since the restaurant had been closed for some time? Something in a can?

It was late. The soldiers would be gone, nonetheless Mick crept down the stairs, should one of them still be lurking about. Once in the kitchen he remembered that he had seen someone disappear behind a cabinet that had appeared to be flush against the wall. Or again, had he been hallucinating from hunger and a lack of sleep? He examined the cabinet more closely. It was moveable. He moved it aside and behind it was a doorway with steps leading down into a tunnel-like hallway that was faintly lighted by a single yellow bulb hanging on a cord from the ceiling. He descended the steps, and at the end of the tunnel he could see a room, also faintly lit, that contained racks of bottles of wine.

"A nice glass of wine would taste good right now," Mick said to himself. He proceeded on into the room, and to his utter shock, he came face-to-face with a woman. She gasped and started to run. Mick grabbed her.

"Wait, I won't hurt you."

She struggled to get away.

"Are you Lovea Duval?"

"Let me go!"

"Listen, I won't harm you, I'm on your side. I work for the CIA. I'm an American."

She stopped struggling.

"The CIA?"

Mick quickly explained what his role was, then he asked if she had a cork screw to open a bottle of wine.

"I haven't had a drink since I left Rangoon," he said. "I could use one."

"Yes, of course, would you like some food? I have rice."

"Yes, thank you, I'm very hungry too."

Lovea uncorked a bottle of wine and dished out a bowl of rice with some kind of meat in it.

Mick gobbled some down.

"It's very good. What is it? The meat I mean."

"Lizard. They are plentiful down here."

Mick gulped.

"How long have you been down here, Lovea?"

"Since the Khmer Rouge came in April. How long ago is that now? I've lost track. What month is this?

"October. Do you have enough food to last much longer?"

"One half sack of rice left. That's 50 pounds."

"What will you do when you run out?"

"Drink some wine each day. There is nourishment in that," she said half-seriously. "Would you like some now?"

"Oh yes."

Lovea went to the racks and dusted off a bottle. She held it up to the light. "1939, *Beaujolais.*"

"That year doesn't exist anymore," Mick said.

"What do you mean?"

"Pol Pot has declared 1975 Year Zero. Kampuchea, as Cambodia is now called, has no history before the Communist takeover."

"What else has he done?" Lovea asked.

"Sent all inhabitants of the cities to the countryside where they live in labor camps and grow rice. He has slain thousands more who don't cooperate, and he is killing anyone with ties to the French."

"My father was French. If they find me they will kill me, too. They killed my mother because she would not tell them where I was. They were looking for me, no doubt, to kill me because of my anti-Communist writings. They will do the same to you if they find out you're with the CIA."

"I know. I think they suspect me already, and a man named Pich Sabay, because we went together to see the mass grave at Kmpong Cham without the soldiers."

"More wine?" Lovea asked.

"Yes, it warms my stomach."

Mick was getting light-headed from drinking it and he wanted the high to continue because he hadn't felt so good for some time.

The wine Lovea consumed didn't seem to affect her that much. She was quite sober in her assessment of the predicament in which she found herself, having to hide in the cellar until she died from starvation. What choice did she have? There was no escaping it.

"Well, Lovea, it's time for me to go upstairs and get some sleep. Sabay may be coming early in the morning to take me on a trip to Takeo to see the school where young and old are taught the new way, a euphemism for being brainwashed.

"I'll come back to see you."

"Be very careful that the soldiers don't follow," she said.

"I'll come back late at night when they're not around."

Chapter 8

Sabay came early the next day.

"We can go to Takeo now," he said. "The soldiers are waiting downstairs to escort us."

On the way in the car, Mick told him about discovering Lovea Duval in the hotel wine cellar.

"She's in good spirits considering that she's trapped," Mick said. "There's nowhere she can go. She sneaks water from the kitchen, but she's running low on rice. It's just a matter of time before she either has to come up or stay down there and starve. Either way she is doomed I'm afraid."

"So it seems, so it seems," Sabay said with sad resignation.

Thinking that Mick was a Communist too, the Khmer Rouge allowed him to sit in on a lesson at the school in Takeo. The first thing he noticed upon entering the open-air classroom was a list of rules for the attendees to follow, written in Cambodian of which Mick had learned enough to read, roughly.

1. *You must answer accordingly to my questions, don't turn them away.*

2. *Don't try to hide the facts by making pretexts of this and that. Your are strictly prohibited to contest me.*

3. *Don't be a fool for you are a chap who dare to thwart the revolution.*

4. *You must immediately answer my questions without wasting time to reflect.*

5. *While getting lashes or electrification you must not cry at all.*

6. *Do nothing. Sit still and wait for my orders. If there is no order, keep quiet. When I ask you to do something you must do it right away without protesting.*

7. *If you don't follow all of the rules, you will get many many lashes of electric wire.*

8. *If you protest or contest anything that I tell you you will be taken away never to be heard of again.*

And he knew enough Cambodian to understand most of what the instructor (a little man wearing the black uniform of the Khmer Rouge with its signature red and white scarf) was teaching. The lesson focused on the basic tenets of Communism. Some of the key points being:

* *the abolition of private property*

* *the abolition of the bourgeoisie or middle class (which is defined as a broad group encompassing Capitalists, noble landowners and officials, shopkeepers, prosperous peasants, the intelligencia, doctors, lawyers and teachers, and entrepreneurs in general.*

* *the bringing into cultivation all wastelands, and the improvement of the soil in accordance with a common plan, which in Cambodia would be the pursuit of an agrarian utopia.*

* *the combination of agriculture with industry, and the abolition of the distinction between town and country by a more equitable distribution of the population over the countryside.*

The stern-faced instructor held up a paperback copy of the *Communist Manifesto*, as several copies were being distributed to the attendees by his assistant.

"Remember, as you read this, that bourgeois private property is the final and most complete expression of the system of producing and appropriating products that is based on class antagonisms, on the exploitation of the many by the few. In this sense, the theory of Communism may be summed up in a single phrase: abolition of private property which will then be shared equally by the proletariat, or peasantry, of which you all are now members."

Many attending the class were of the middle class, who had owned private property in the city, and they didn't look that happy about sharing it equally with their proletariat neighbors who owned nothing. But they dared not protest, as the Khmer Rouge ruled with a heavy hand holding a gun, and with no compunction about using it, as Mick had witnessed at Kampong Luong.

"The immediate aim of Communism stated in this *Manifesto* is the same as that of all other peasant revolutions: the formation of the peasantry into a class, the overthrow of the bourgeoisie, and the conquest of political power by the peasantry, which is what the Khmer Rouge has done!"

And the instructor emphasized, perhaps for the benefit of Mick, who he thought was a Soviet, that Russia's great Lenin-led Bolshevik Revolution was won by peasant soldiers like the Khmer Rouge who fought to assure the common ownership and stewardship of the land by the peasants of Kampuchea in order to attain an agrarian utopia -- the dream of Pol Pot.

"However, I must emphasize that our revolution is fashioned more after the narodniki's form of peasant-oriented Communism which was pre-industrial, pre-Marxist and pre-Leninist. It focused heavily on the development of a mass agricultural society in which the people -- all of the people -- participated in working the land as opposed to slaving away in the factories of the cities as human machines producing obscene profits for the bourgeoisie while the proletariat lived in abject poverty.

"No! No more in Kampuchea!" The instructor had worked himself up into a frenzy. His brown face turned red; his eyes grew wild.

"We will live off the land where all profit equally. The Khmer Rouge has done this by casting off the shackles of French colonialism that enslaved the common farmer. And led by Pol Pot, they have liberated the people of Kampuchea from the pro-Western bourgeoisie puppet Lon Nol!"

And Mick understood enough Cambodian to know what an older man said when he stood up and shouted that Pol Pot was a bloody tyrant who was enslaving his own people by forcing them into gulag-like labor camps.

He was immediately dragged away kicking and screaming. Soon afterward Mick heard the shots. Indeed, he had been taken away never to be heard of again as promised in rule #8.

The lesson continued as if nothing unusual had happened. When it was finished, one of the soldiers, who Mick concluded was the leader of the contingent that had escorted him to Takeo, approached, smiling.

"Radio Moscow would like to hear what was said here today, especially about Russian Revolution being like Khmer Rouge revolution, no? Man who protested will not he heard though, yes?" He stopped smiling.

But instead of reporting favorably on the school's teachings of Communism for Radio Moscow, Mick went back to his hotel room and recorded the following for Voice of America.

On the road to Takeo I saw the masses slaving in the sun growing rice for the Man, Pol Pot. City-dwellers from all walks of life, forced to become farmers overnight. Capitalists one day, Communists the next. They were being called the New People, as opposed to the Old People, who made up the peasantry that had roots in the countryside where the Khmer Rouge were born.

In schools like the one at Takeo, all New People would learn quickly the new way, or be imprisoned or shot. It was that simple, that brutal, that cut and dried. I watched as an older man who questioned what was being taught was dragged from the school by a young soldier not much older than 17. From a distance I heard the shot.

There is no respect for recent history any more. As decreed by Pol Pot, everything begins with 1975, the Year Zero, the year Cambodia became known as Kampuchea, when the Khmer Rouge took over and initiated a peasant-based revolution fashioned after the narodniki or populist form of pre-industrial Russian Communism pre-dating Marx and Engel and Lenin and the Bolshevik Revolution. While the Bolsheviks saw the urban workers as the great revolutionary class, the Party of Socialist-Revolutionaries of the narodniki tradition held the peasantry in higher regard and believed that it embodied the egalitarian and communal values at the heart of socialism or Communism.

And in schools like the one at Takeo, the New People are being brainwashed; those who resist end up in mass graves.

Chapter 9

Sabay came to Mick's room out of breath, disheveled and looking very frightened.

"Before I could get your last tape to Lam Linh on the runway the soldiers grabbed me and took me to the offices of the Ministry of Information and played it on a recorder. They know now that you are reporting for Voice of America, not Radio Moscow. When they left me alone for a moment, I escaped through a window. They will be coming soon; we must go to the airport immediately and fly to Rangoon with Lam Linh. He will be on the runway still waiting for me, but not for much longer, we must hurry. We will have to run, my car is at the airport."

"I'm going to take Lovea with us," Mick insisted.

They rushed out of the room and down to the kitchen. Mick pushed the cabinet aside descended the steps to the tunnel and shouted.

"Lovea, the soldiers are coming for me and Sabay. This is your chance to escape, come with us to the airport, now before the plane leaves. We will fly together to Rangoon. Hurry, please, come with us, Lovea!"

She ran up the tunnel to Mick. "Yes, yes, let's go!"

The three ran out onto the street. No Khmer Rouge were in sight -- until Mick looked back just before they turned a corner, and saw a Jeep with four soldiers in it speeding up to the hotel. It didn't appear that the soldiers saw them.

Sabay knew the way to the airport through a maze of obscure side streets.

"It's three miles. We can make it, if we run, in 30 or 40 minutes. Hopefully Lam Linh will still be on the ground waiting for me to give him the tape," Sabay said as they ran. But then the unforseen occurred.

A Khmer Rouge armored personnel carrier rumbled onto the side street on which the three were running. No soldiers were visible on top of the vehicle, but had the ones inside seen them through the small rectangular window in the front?

Sabay grabbed Mick and he in turn grabbed Lovea and they ducked into an alley. A burst of machine gun fire raked the corner of the building they'd ducked behind. Mick felt debris spatter the back of his head and neck, stinging like bees. The bullet had come so close that he smelled burnt plaster. Luckily, the alley led to another, perpendicular to the one into which they had run. No APC could traverse it, but, of course, the soldiers could; by the time they dismounted, the three had lost them in the maze, through which Sabay knew the way to the airport that was, according to his estimate, only a mile away now.

They moved along at a trot. Sabay, an older man, grew winded. They stopped to rest until they heard excited voices approaching. Mick tried the door of a house near where they stopped. It was unlocked. They went in. The place was abandoned, as many houses in the capital were, the inhabitants having been relocated to the countryside. They pushed a heavy piece of furniture against the door. Running footsteps went by. Soon they deemed it was safe to move again. They were only about six blocks from the airport, Sabay said, and they covered that quickly. No soldiers appeared to be there. They ran through the front door past the unmanned customs desk, out the back and onto the runway. Lam Linh had started his engines and was beginning to taxi for take off. They ran for the plane shouting and waving. Lovea stumbled and fell. Mick went back to help her up and he saw soldiers coming out the back of the airport terminal, rifles poised to shoot. The plane was rolling away slowly, then it stopped. The side door opened and Tran Van, the co-pilot, helped the three on board as the soldiers peppered the plane with gunfire. Sabay was hit in the left buttock. He fell forward in the aisle between the seats bleeding. Tran Van rushed to his side with a first aid kit.

"Bullet came out inside of his upper thigh. Bleed bad."

Tran Van pressed a patch of gauze into the exit wound that was exposed through the hole in Sabay's pants, and held it in place with tape which he managed to wrap between his legs and around his waist.

Meanwhile Lam Linh had taken off, but altitude came slowly. There was something wrong with the plane. It barely kept aloft above the trees. Mick looked out one of the windows, it was splattered with oil. Through it he could see the left engine propellor stalling. Tran Van came back again.

"Strap into your seats, we may have to ditch in a rice paddy before we come to the mountains."

Mick and Lovea helped Sabay into one of the seats and strapped him in. He moaned from the pain of his wound. Then they strapped themselves in. They could hear the sound of the damaged engine sputtering beneath the drone of the good one. The plane vibrated, flying slightly askew. From where he sat, Mick saw Lam Linh in the cockpit fighting to keep the plane under control while pulling back hard on the wheel to maintain altitude -- to no avail: the plane was going down slowly. Mick looked out the window again. They were flying low over an expanse of wetlands adjacent to a huge lake. It would be a relatively soft belly-flop landing, Mick thought, but they hit with a jarring jolt. Water splashed up on the windows. After bouncing two or three times they came to an abrupt stop. Lam Linh and Tran Van came rushing back, opened the door and looked around.

"No see any Khmer Rouge. Hurry to those trees," Lam Linh said. "We must hide."

Mick and Tran Van lifted Sabay down to Lam Linh and Lovea who were standing in knee-deep water. Once down, Mick threw Sabay, a thin, light man, over his shoulder and the four of them plodded as fast as they could to the trees which turned out to be thick jungle. They went about fifty yards in and laid Sabay down. Lam Linh took a radio from his flight suit.

"I don't know how close we are to Thailand, but I know they still have a U.S. Air Force para-rescue squadron stationed at Udorn that's used to search for the wreckage of U.S. planes shot down during the Vietnam War in hopes of finding missing airmen and their remains. If I could contact them on this maybe they could get a chopper to us."

"Look!" Tran Van shouted. "Out there, beyond where we went down; pagodas, towering pagodas, must be Angkor Wat. If so, rescue crew would know where we are! Not so far from Thailand!"

"Yes, I'll call May Day," Lam Linh said.

Sabay began to moan again. Tran Van attended to him then he motioned for Mick, Lam Linh and Lovea to come with him a few feet away. He whispered. "Losing lots of blood. Very pale, about to pass out. Needs to be rescued fast."

Lam Linh clicked the radio. "Calling Udorn Air Force Base. May Day, May Day. DC-3 shot down by Khmer Rouge near Angkor Wat shrine, Cambodia. Five aboard, one badly wounded. Over." He repeated the transmission.

"We must go to the pagodas for rescue," Tran Van said. "Take turns to carry Sabay. Be careful of cobras, Khmer Rouge. Same, same, both very deadly."

Lam Linh called Udorn on the radio again, before they set out.

"We'll probably have to spend the night at the pagodas," Tran Van said. "I doubt if rescue would be possible before dark, even if they hear us, Udorn is too far away."

They sloshed through the knee-deep waters of the wetland for a good two miles, Mick and Tran Van taking turns carrying Sabay while Lam Linh periodically radioed Udorn. Still no response.

Finally they came to the higher, dry land. They laid Sabay down. He was barely conscious and still losing blood. His pants were soaked with it. Lovea rested his head on her lap. He exhaled, went limp and died. Sabay's death brought great sadness to Mick who had grown close to him, living together in danger as they had. Mick cried, not outwardly but deep inside. He fought back the tears, not wanting to appear too soft when fortitude was a must. The fortitude to carry on.

"We can't leave him here. I'll carry him to the pagodas."

Mick draped Sabay's limp, bloodied body over his shoulder and they trudged on.

As they neared Angkor Wat the towering pagodas' magnificence and intricacy became more apparent. Their ornate facades, some with the gigantic faces of Buddhas, and statues of figures depicting ancient Cambodian lore, were smudged by time and mold, having been overgrown by the jungle for centuries, until French archaeologists began uncovering and restoring the shrines. Lovea's father had been one of the Frenchmen who helped to reclaim the temples from the jungle. She stood proudly in awe of the sight, smiling. Her eyes grew moist. A tear streamed down her cheek.

"My father was very proud of what he did here for the people of Cambodia."

They crossed a bridge spanning a wide moat that surrounded the temple of Angkor Wat. At the entrance Mick laid Sabay's body down gently as Lovea pointed out a delicately carved bas-relief of female celestial dancers on a long wall, "Depicting the glorious lore of the 12th Century Khmer Empire; goddesses dancing for the kings," she said.

They were pock-marked by bullets depicting modern Cambodia's ever-present state of war.

"My father brought me here when I was a young girl. He told me the temple was originally dedicated to the Hindu god Vishnu around 900 A.D. but over the centuries it became a Buddhist shrine as the Khmer kings no longer worshiped Hindu gods and Buddhism, long-popular with the masses, became the sole faith."

Mick stepped back and looked up at the lotus-shaped central tower of Angkor Wat, flanked by other similar towers that appeared to rise to a height of a least 200 feet from where he stood.

"Magnificent," he said.

"Yes, the towers represent the peaks of Mt. Meru, the Olympus of Hindu gods and center of the universe where Brahma the creator god resides," Lovea said.

"This would be a good place to bury Sabay," Mick said. "Problem is we don't have anything to dig with."

"Cremate," Lam Linh said. He smoked, so he had matches, kept dry in one of the breast pockets of his flight suit. He held them up. "First we must find dry wood."

The thought of burning Sabay's body didn't sit well with Mick, but it was a tradition among some Buddhists, of which Sabay was one.

Before they set about finding wood, Lam Linh made another May Day call on the radio. This time he got a response, although the transmission was full of static and barely audible, but he could make out that Udorn Air Base had received his earlier call and they asked him to repeat the scenario.

"DC-3 shot down near Tonle Sap lake northeast. Four survivors at nearby Angkor Wat shrine, over."

There was a brief transmission in return then the radio went dead. Lam Linh slapped it several times in the palm of his hand hoping to make it work again, but it didn't.

"We can only hope they received my last transmission. All we can do now is wait until morning. They would not come at night. Meanwhile we will make a big fire for Sabay. Must be very hot to burn his body to ash. Brown bamboo burns beaucoup hot. Lovea, I see that there is a grove of banana palms and fig trees around the bend of the moat. Could you try to find some to eat. I'll gather palm leaves to make for our bed, Mick and Tran Van, you two gather dead bamboo for fire."

Lam Linh had assumed the leadership role, and for the first time Mick noticed how much he resembled the handsome, mustached Nguyen Cao Ky, the former hotshot fighter pilot and vice president of South Vietnam, who had been a great leader in his own right. And Tran Van could have passed for his brother, minus the mustache.

Mick and Tran Van found an abundance of bamboo for the fire.

"Criss-cross and pile high for Sabay's body to lay on," Tran Van instructed Mick. "We'll use brown palm leaves for kindling. They break off the trees easily."

Lovea found plenty of ripe bananas and figs and they ate, then Lam Linh lit the fire, and Mick and Tran Van placed Sabay's body on the bed of bamboo. Mick took a walk, not wanting to witness the cremation. He went upwind and sat on a stone at the base of a pagoda. Soon, in the distance, near where their plane had gone down, he caught a glimpse of the tiny silhouettes of a column of men walking. Could they be Khmer Rouge? If so, could they see the smoke of the fire? If it got dark soon enough perhaps they wouldn't. Mick watched them for awhile. They appeared to be coming his way, but they were still a good distance away. As the sun went down it became more difficult to see them. Mick went back to the others to tell them what he had seen.

"Now that it's dark, they'll not advance any further," Lam Linh said. "They'll camp for the night."

The flames of the fire had died down into bits of glowing embers. Sabay's cremation was complete. Lovea, Lam Linh and Tran Van blessed the ashes with a Buddhist incantation.

A half moon shed enough light for Mick to see where Lam Linh had put down the palm leaves for bedding. He laid down and Lovea cuddled up next to him and she quickly fell asleep.

The black sky above was filled with bright sparkling stars. As tired as he was, Mick could not sleep. He worried about how close the Khmer Rouge had come before dark, and he wondered if Udorn had received enough of their last distress call to locate them if a rescue could be undertaken. Would it come down to a race with the Khmer Rouge to reach them if Udorn had received the call?

Gradually Mick fell asleep, comforted by Lovea's sweet breathing in his ear. She was at peace, and at least free from her trap at the hotel in Phnom Penh.

Chapter 10

Awakened by the first light of dawn, Mick got to his feet and stretched. It took a moment for him to recall everything about the predicament he was in. He looked down at Lovea. She had awakened too and was getting up. Lam Linh and Tran Van had been up and they were standing nearby smoking cigarettes.

"Come let's see where the soldiers are," Lam Linh said.

They went to the clearing from where Mick had seen them walking near the plane the day before. The soldiers were closer now, but they were gathered around a pillar of smoke.

"Cooking fire. They're having breakfast," Tran Van said.

"Me too." Mick peeled one of the bananas Lovea had found and he devoured it. The others ate one too.

They sat in silence and watched the soldiers for a while. If they had spotted the smoke of Sabay's cremation fire, which had long died into ashes, they didn't seem in any hurry to find its source, as they sat around their cooking fire eating, but then suddenly they became very animated.

"Listen," Tran Van said, half-whispering. "I think I hear a chopper. Yes, look, out there!"

Mick saw a black dot in the sky. It gradually grew larger. Judging from its sound it was definitely a chopper. He took note of the soldiers. They had advanced toward Angkor Wat considerably, moving at a hurried pace as the chopper's appearance became more distinct. Mick recognized it from the Vietnam War as one of the infamous Jolly Green Giant rescue helicopters. The four of them began to wave wildly as it circled in over their position. The Khmer Rouge were approaching the bridge that spanned the moat. They began firing at the Jolly Green, which returned fire with the .60 caliber machine gun, pinning the soldiers down. The chopper hovered above while sending down a cable with a paramedic in a harness. He got out and helped Lovea in, and she was hoisted swiftly into the belly of Jolly Green, then it was Mick's turn, followed by Tran Van and the captain of the sunken ship, Lam Linh. All the while the door gunner kept firing at the Khmer Rouge, who couldn't get off a shot during the entire rescue. Only after the chopper began to leave the area did Mick see them shooting, but apparently they were only good marksmen if they shot an unarmed peasant in the head at point-blank range.

It was a relatively short flight to Udorn, a base that during the Vietnam War had served as a launching pad for US Air Force fighter bombers attacking North Vietnam. Many had been shot down and Jolly Green crews saved as many of the downed pilots as they could, sometimes getting shot down themselves, which was nearly the case at Angkor Wat. The pilot counted seven bullet holes in the chopper, but none had hit anything crucial to flight, and, more importantly, the crew and the rescued. They all stood on the flight line and hugged. Lovea kissed everyone on the cheek. She was tasting freedom for the first time in nearly two years.

After a meal of baked chicken in the base chow hall (the first meat Mick had had in months, besides lizard) they were put on a C-130 headed for Bangkok.

Mick had enough money to put the four of them up in a hotel in Bangkok. He and Lovea in separate rooms and Lam Linh and Tran Van together. They had the maid wash and dry their clothes in the hotel laundry room. As soon as they dressed again they met in the hotel bar for libations in celebration of their escape from Phnom Penh.

It was the best-tasting cold beer Mick had ever had. Lam Linh and Tran Van had beer too, and Lovea had wine. They drank a toast to Sabay, who had risked his life taking tapes to Lam Linh at Phnom Penh's airport, and they toasted to Lam Linh and Tran Van for flying the tapes out of Cambodia to Burma, and they toasted the Jolly Green rescue crew in absentia, and they toasted Lovea for her freedom, and Mick for exposing the Khmer Rouge atrocities to the rest of the world through Voice of America, and by the time they finished all the toasting which kept the bartender busy, they were pleasantly drunk.

"So what will you do now?" Mick asked Lam Linh.

"I don't know. Maybe I will go to the US of A. I hear they need bush pilots in Alaska. If I can land in a lake, surely I can land on ice and snow."

"Don't ask me to be your copilot," Tran Van said. "Too cold up there for Vietnamese like me. Not an Eskimo. I'll go to Los Angeles where it is warm."

"What about you, Mick?" Lam Linh asked.

"I'll fly to Rangoon to touch base with Voice of America, then I'll go back home to Carbondale, Illinois. And you Lovea? What are your plans?"

She suddenly became sober. Her eyes flared. "To avenge my mother's murder, and the murder of many others."

"How will you manage to do that?"

"By organizing a counterinsurgency and going back to Cambodia to kill Khmer Rouge."

"Would men follow a woman into battle?" Tran Van asked.

"Yes. My father taught me about Joan of Arc. How she led French forces to victory at Orleans in the Hundred Years War when the English occupied France."

"I'm sure you could find many volunteers among the thousands of refugees who have fled across the Cambodian border into Thailand," Lam Linh said, encouraging Lovea.

"There is a Colonel Yon I know of who led the counter attack at Oudong that routed the Khmer Rouge. When Phnom Penh finally fell, he went into exile to Bangkok with some of his officers. Surely he would be willing to help, Lam Linh. If they sought political asylum, someone in the Thai government may know exactly where he is in Bangkok."

"Oh yes, Colonel Yon. I knew of him from the hotel. Occasionally he and his men came there to drink wine. He teased me about the muscles in my arms when I carried the trays of drinks to their table. He said I should be a soldier in his army," Lovea said.

"Maybe you will be, or he in yours if your plans come true," Lam Linh said.

"Who should I talk to, Lam Linh, in the Thai government to help me find the Colonel?" Lovea asked.

"Someone with Immigration & Customs I would think. It may be confidential information though. But a few well-placed greenbacks could open a file, say in the hands of a clerk I know at the airport who works for Immigration & Customs. His name is Nakhon."

Mick counted out fifty dollars in greenbacks and placed them on the table.

"Will this help, Lam Linh?"

"Perhaps. In the morning I will go to the airport."

Chapter 11

Lam Linh waited until no one else was around, then he dropped the fifty bucks on Nakhon.

"I'm looking for a Cambodian, a Colonel Yon, who possibly has sought political asylum. It is believed that he is in Bangkok somewhere."

Nakhon raised his eyebrows at the sight of the money and smiled. "I'll see what I can find. Come back this afternoon."

Lam Linh returned at four. Nakhon slipped him a piece of paper with an address on it – 435 Sattahip Street. He called Lovea's room on the hotel phone. "Meet me in the lounge. I have something for you," he said.

"Okay. I'll bring Mick and Tran Van too."

Lam Linh presented Lovea with the address of Colonel Yon.

"Just show this to the taxi cab driver."

"Okay. I will first thing in the morning. In the meantime I'd like to go next door and buy a new outfit to meet the Colonel in. Something not so feminine as this dress."

"Yes, Lovea looked very feminine in the dress," Mick thought, although it had been awhile since she had shaved her legs: looking quite French after all.

"I agree," Lam Linh said. "If you are wanting to present yourself as a soldier maybe it is not best to do it in a dress, and one so lovely, I might add."

Knowing she had no money, Mick offered to buy her the clothes. He had a plentiful supply of US dollars.

She chose a manly-looking khaki pant suit and men's boots to downplay her femininity. If she were to try to convince the Colonel that she could lead a counterinsurgency, she wanted to look the part.

In the morning Mick went with her in a cab to find Colonel Yon. The address turned out to be a villa tucked away on an alley-like street in the shade of a palm grove. The property was surrounded by a high stone wall with a wrought iron gate. They got out of the cab and peered through the gate which was padlocked.

"Hello, is anyone here?" Lovea called out. "Hello, Colonel Yon? It is Prey Lovea Duval from the Hotel Angkor in Phnom Penh."

Soon a dark-complected man in a white suit with a mustache and goatee, looking very much like a "Kentucky Colonel," but younger, appeared on the veranda.

"Yes," he said. "Lovea. I remember you well. You have escaped Cambodia. Let me unlock the gate."

The Colonel came out and put a key to the lock and swung the gate open.

"Colonel Yon, this is Mick Scott of America. He escaped with me."

"An American in Phnom Penh?"

"I was posing as a Russian reporter for Radio Moscow"

"Surprised they let you there. The Khmer Rouge is very wary of Soviets. They are close allies of Vietnam and the Khmer Rouge are at odds with the Vietnamese these days."

"Yes, well, they thought I'd be reporting favorably on Cambodia's form of Communism to impress the Kremlin so they would possibly provide arms to them, but instead I reported on the atrocities for Voice of America."

The Colonel nodded and smiled.

"Well I am glad to see you Lovea. To what do I owe the honor of this visit?"

"May we go inside and talk?"

"Of course. Come this way."

They entered the house. Colonel Yon led the way through a large living room and into the kitchen.

"I've just put on a pot of tea," the Colonel said. "Please, sit down at the table. I'll pour some when it's ready. Meanwhile let's have some bread fresh from the bakery. It's very good with this lemon marmalade."

The Colonel put the bread on a cutting board on the table and sliced it, and spread the marmalade on each piece.

"The tea is ready. They go very well together. Now, tell me Lovea, why have you come?"

"To ask you to help me lead an insurgency against the Khmer Rouge."

"You are not the first to think of this. The CIA has contacted me in the past to see if I would be interested. They offered to provide arms and ammunition if I found enough people to join me and other ex-patriots from the army, and refugees who have settled along the Thai border with Cambodia. We would train select refugees to fight. You would be interested in fighting, Lovea?"

"Yes, they murdered my mother."

"They have murdered many, some say close to a million by now. They must be stopped, but we cannot do it without weapons. You have inspired me, Lovea. We will get in touch with a man I know who works for the CIA immediately to see what can be done. Come with me to the US Embassy today. Mick, you may stay here until we return, drink more tea, eat bread and marmalade, listen to Voice of America on the radio. Maybe you will hear yourself," the Colonel joked.

At that moment a man with slicked-back black hair and a mustache entered the room, looking sleepy.

"Oh, this is my cousin, Ing Pech," the Colonel said. "He's been upstairs taking a nap, what you call a beauty rest. He will be happy to keep you company, Mick, while we are gone. He is interested in forming a counterinsurgency too, having been subjected to much Khmer Rouge brutality in the prison at Tuol Sleng before he escaped after enduring two long years of torture."

"Yes." Ing, despite being reminded of what he had gone through, managed a polite smile and he shook hands with Mick.

"And this is Lovea Duval, Ing," the Colonel said introducing the two.

Ing bowed and took Lovea's hand and kissed it. "I have long wanted to meet you. I am very familiar with your writings."

"Oh," she said, smiling shyly.

After Colonel Yon and Lovea left, Mick took the liberty of asking Ing about the transgression that had landed him in prison.

"I am a teacher."

"You were imprisoned because you were a teacher?"

"Yes, very ironic when you consider that Pol Pot himself was a teacher at a secondary school in Phnom Penh. I taught secondary English and French, which the Khmer Rouge considered to be the language of imperialists who have plundered countries like Cambodia. But it is they who are plundering their own country, and worst yet committing the genocide of their own people. It must stop. The United States or the United Nations must intervene, but of all people it is rumored that the Vietnamese soon will invade us with the intention of deposing Pol Pot, who they fear will invade them. In fact, the Khmer Rouge have launched probes into Vietnam's territory. They in turn have attacked Khmer Rouge inside Cambodian territory. If all-out war erupts, the people of Cambodia will be caught in between.

"In the final analysis, it is we who must rise up and resist Pol Pot with a counterinsurgency like the one being proposed by Lovea Duval, if we are ever to be free of the Khmer Rouge and the Vietnamese who are both Communist oppressors."

"How did you escape, Ing?"

"By feigning death while lying among dead bodies that were dumped in a pit outside the prison."

Chapter 12

Colonel Yon was able to meet with his man at the CIA immediately. They knew who he was from past discussions about forming a counterinsurgency to be deployed in Cambodia against the Khmer Rouge. Agent Don Young, a tall, slender, balding man greeted him with open arms.

"And this is your daughter, Colonel?" Young asked.

"No, this is Prey Lovea Duval. She escaped from Cambodia but she wants to return with me to fight the Khmer Rouge."

"Why not? In Vietnam many young women fought for the Viet Cong. Down through the ages Vietnamese women are well-known for fighting for their country," Young pointed out.

"The legendary Trung sisters led an insurrection against occupying Chinese in A.D. 40, and in the 3rd century Trieu Au launched a revolt against China while riding an elephant into battle ahead of a thousand men. So you would not be the first Southeast Asian woman to do as much, Miss Duval.

"Now, to begin with ...," Young said, motioning to chairs for them to sit on, and he pulled one around from behind his desk and they sat in a circle, "...you'll need weapons of course, and the U.S. Air Force has a surplus of them that were used by their security police in guarding the various air bases throughout Thailand during the war. They are being stockpiled at Udorn where the U.S. still supports a base."

"I'm very familiar with Udorn Air Base," Lovea said. "They sent one of their rescue helicopters to extract me and my friends from a very precarious situation in Cambodia recently."

"They are sill involved in searching for missing American airmen from the war. At any rate, these surplus weapons could be secured for your purposes with a little creative manipulation of inventory accountability, so to speak, which would show that the surplus has been procured in accordance with agency guidelines regarding the sponsorship of insurgents in developing countries where Communism is a threat to the well-being of a populace. Something that could easily be justified in Cambodia," Young said, speaking fluent CIA bureaucratese, which was understandable since he had "come in from the cold" and was manning a desk. But his proposal to "cook the books," as it were, through creative manipulation of inventory accountability, was certainly welcomed by Colonel Yon and Lovea.

"In the meantime we could recruit refugees in the camps along the border by distributing pamphlets explaining the mission," Colonel Yon suggested.

"They can be trained at a Thai military base near Aranyaprathet, which is just across the border from Poipet, Cambodia, where tens of thousands of refugees have gathered," Young said.

"Three other combat-experienced officers who sought political asylum with me would help train," the Colonel said with mounting enthusiasm.

"You could possibly enlist the assistance of Thai officers also," Young offered. "Thailand has a vested interest in keeping the Khmer Rouge at bay, or to be more exact, eliminating them altogether, as they pose an immediate threat on their southeastern frontier.

"The pamphlets, Colonel Yon, how should they read? We will design and print them here."

"Let's see now." The Colonel thought for a moment.

"*Bear arms, return to Cambodia, liberate the oppressed. Join us at Aranyaprathet to train under Colonel Yon and Lovea Duval.* Your name, Lovea, would be famous among many of the refugees who are astute politically and were aware of your anti-Communist columns. When Agent Young, when could we begin training?"

"As soon as possible, let's say in five weeks or so. That's enough time to design, print and distribute the pamphlets and coordinate plans with the Thais to use their training facilities at Aranyaprathet. It will take longer to get the weapons, though -- maybe three months. You'll have to train without them for a while."

"How would you suggest we distribute the pamphlets?" the Colonel asked.

"We'll have Air America fly over the refugee camps and release them," Young said.

"So then, the plan has been set in motion," Lovea said.

"Yes, it will gain momentum as the days pass," Young said. "Keep in touch with me at least every three or four days."

Colonel Yon and Lovea shook hands with Agent Young to finalize the deal. If all went well, within six months they'd be in action against the Khmer Rouge, employing guerrilla tactics to harass them and to kill them, wherever they were.

Back at the villa, where Mick and Ing had been waiting and listening to Voice of America report on the continuous bloodbath in Cambodia, Colonel Yon poured wine to celebrate what had transpired with the CIA. It had all happened so fast -- at least as far as the preliminary plans were concerned. But it would be a while before they were put into action.

"I must go now, Lovea, to catch a plane to Rangoon." Mick stood. Lovea's filled with tears. She stood and they hugged, and Mick kissed her on the cheek.

"If it weren't for you I'd still be living in that dungeon in Phnom Penh," she said, wiping the tears from her eyes, "living on lizards." She smiled.

"What will you do now, Mick, after you've gone to Rangoon?"

"Go back to Illinois. I've got a dog and a cat and a girl friend waiting there for me. It's been more than a year and a half since I've seen them. I've almost forgotten what they look like. Goodbye Lovea and Colonel Yon, Ing. Good luck, and may the gods of Angkor Wat be with you."

"Goodbye, Mick," Lovea said sadly.

"Goodbye." The Colonel shook Mick's hand.

Chapter 13

Lam Linh and Tran Van took jobs at the Bangkok airport handling baggage, but they planned to go to the U.S. as soon as they could afford it. Lam Linh was serious about becoming a bush pilot in Alaska, and Tran Van was just as serious about going to L.A. where it was warmer, and there was a substantial population of Vietnamese expatriates.

Mick went on to Rangoon. Monroe was shocked to see him in person at the Voice of America studios, having expected to receive a tape from him in Cambodia instead. Mick explained that the Khmer Rouge had intercepted his last one and subsequently he and Sabay were shot down in Lam Linh's plane trying to escape Phnom Penh, with Sabay eventually dying in the process before being rescued.

"Thank God you made it out! If they'd caught you they surely would have killed you. Too bad about Sabay. He was a good soldier."

Monroe paused, providing an impromptu moment of silence. "And your tapes, Mick, they helped to shed light on the terrible nightmare that's occurring there. So what are your plans now?"

"To go back home and fatten up on spaghetti and meat balls, garlic bread and beer. I'm starving."

"Yes, you look thin."

"There is very little food in Cambodia, people are dying of starvation."

"How would you like to take another assignment before you go back home? This time you'd be working as a Voice of America correspondent up front, and not under the guise of a Russian reporting for Radio Moscow. You'd be returning to Vietnam with an American task force that's going there to recover the remains of missing in action from the war."

"Sounds like an exhausting task. Some of those guys went missing deep in the jungles of mountainous Laos, where we weren't supposed to be, I might add, although enemy activity, particularly on the Ho Chi Minh Trail, called for it," Mick said.

"Yes. As a result a few American boys went missing there, where the Trail comes from Laos, across the very northeastern tip of Cambodia and into Vietnam in the Central Highlands. It's an area known as the Bermuda Triangle of M.I.A.s," Monroe said. "However, the first leg of the mission would entail going north of the old DMZ to search for the remains of missing pilots. You'd start off in Hanoi, then head south to the Central Highlands.

"Intriguing. I'm surprised the Vietnamese are being so congenial as to allow a search for our missing to occur," Mick said.

"Well, at first they demanded that we pay reparations for the damage we inflicted on the country, both North and South, during the war before a delegation would be allowed there, but they've since -- for the time being at least -- relaxed that demand in hopes of some day normalizing relations with the U.S., which could lead to future Congress-authorized humanitarian aid to them."

"When would this assignment begin?" Mick asked.

"Next week. The task force will be stopping over at Clark Air Force Base near Manila before they fly on to Hanoi. You'd meet them there at intelligence headquarters."

"Can you give me a couple of days to decide?"

"Sure."

That night Mick wrote a letter to Kathy saying that it would be another six months or so before he would be back home.

I've taken another assignment with Voice of America accompanying a task force to Vietnam to recover the remains of American troops missing in action. Might as well, since I'm in this part of the world anyway. Besides it's a chance to do my part in bringing some of these guys back home. I was lucky enough to come home. Although I wouldn't be participating in any excavations myself, I'd be publicizing the effort which would be a morale booster to the survivors who are waiting for their loved ones to be repatriated.

Mick flew from Rangoon to Manila on Flying Tiger Airlines and took a shuttle bus to nearby Clark Air Force Base, where he hooked up with the task force at intelligence headquarters, It consisted of five ex-U.S. military men, an anthropologist and a mortician. It was led by Jake Damphier, an American industrialist and philanthropist who was financing the mission.

One of the delegation was Rick Jenkins, a former navy fighter-bomber pilot who had been shot down near the North Vietnamese port of Haiphong, and had been a prisoner of war in the Hanoi Hilton for three years. He bore the scars from his ordeal. One of his ears had been badly mangled by parachute cords when he ejected from the plane, and he had a deformed jaw that had been broken with a club when North Vietnamese peasants discovered him hiding in a hut not far from where he had dropped bombs. It hadn't healed properly because his prison guards constantly cuffed him on the jaw with their fists causing a deformity that his long, thick sideburns almost managed to cover. Jenkins had a vested interest in the mission, besides wanting to find fellow pilots who were missing. His brother-in-law, a U.S. Marine major and platoon leader went missing in the hills surrounding Khe Sanh in 1968. They had both graduated from the Naval Academy in the same class in 1966. At their graduation Jenkins introduced his sister to the Major and they were married in 1967 just before he went to Vietnam. It was now 1977, ten years after she last received a letter in response to her letter, telling him of her pregnancy. They now had a little girl who had never known her father. Jenkins hoped that someday she would. He thought perhaps that the Major was a prisoner of war and still alive, as slim as that possibility was. But first, they would look for remains in and around a bunker on Hill 881, where the Major was last seen, engaged in close combat with the enemy.

Chapter 14

After reunification, Vietnam's dogmatic, no-nonsense government adhered to hard-line Communist principles so stringently that there was no room for any other way of thinking.

"The Communist Party of Vietnam, based on Marxism and Leninism is the only force leading the state and society, and the main factor determining the success of the Vietnamese revolution," read the new constitution drafted for the newly united country that had come to be known as the Socialist Republic of Vietnam.

Reuniting Vietnam had been the goal of Ho Chi Minh and the North Vietnamese Communists, which they achieved as a result of their astounding victory in April of 1975 over South Vietnam, but reconciliation between Northerners and Southerners, civilians and soldiers after the war did not follow easily. Nearly half a million South Vietnamese -- soldiers, teachers, writers, student activists, businessmen and intellectuals, along with some common criminals -- were sent off to reeducation camps where they were brainwashed into thinking like Communists. Those who resisted were confined to cramped wooden boxes, lit by a single light bulb hanging overhead that was kept on all night. A pith helmet in each box served as a toilet. The inhabitants were bound with the right hand tied to the left ankle, the left hand to the right ankle. They were fed two meager bowls of rice a day, if they could manage to eat, bound as they were.

Another two million people were forced into "economic zones" for cooperative farming. In response to these harsh measures, more than a million Vietnamese left their homeland after the Communist takeover of '75. Vietnam's best and brightest -- the writers and scholars, statesmen and economists and merchants -- the people Hanoi would need to build a new nation, sought freedom elsewhere. What remained was a poverty-stricken, isolated nation where just owning a bicycle qualified one for middle-class status. Vietnam was poorer than it had ever been. Food was rationed, and a pair of shoes was beyond the means of most families -- unless they were prominent Party members. The price of rice rose from 30 cents a pound to nearly two dollars. Isolated by international sanctions, including a trade embargo by the U.S., the country survived almost exclusively on Soviet Union aid.

Newspapers ceased publishing, and the bookstores closed. Library shelves were emptied, and more than 100 authors and nearly 1,000 specific titles were banned. Then Hanoi sent nearly 200,000 books to the south -- mostly about Marx, Engels and Lenin heralding Communism, despite the fact it was failing miserably in Vietnam.

When Mick arrived in Hanoi he noticed that the people walking or biking about looked melancholy. They moved around apparently without direction or purpose. It seemed that their only goal was to simply survive, a pitiful state of affairs, considering that Vietnam had been victorious in the American war.

The task force's Vietnamese escort appeared more upbeat though, and he was dressed better than most, with new shoes, a clean white shirt and nice black trousers: perks that went along with being a Communist Party official. His name was Nguyen Xuan. He met the task force at the airport and gave them a quick tour of Hanoi on their way to the villa where they'd meet with other officials to coordinate the search for troops missing in action.

The U.S., contrary to popular belief, had spared most of Hanoi in its bombing. The city's non-military structures survived the war remarkably well, including the magnificent government buildings on Le Thanh Tong Street, which Xuan pointed out proudly, though their architecture was French-inspired. Xuan also pointed put, with even more pride, a B-52 Flying Fortress bomber, remarkably still intact, protruding from the murky waters of a pond in a working-class neighborhood to which he took them. No one else in the neighborhood paid it much attention. They had apparently grown accustomed to seeing the gigantic, well-preserved war trophy.

To the south, not far away, Bach Mai Hospital had barely survived the infamous Christmas bombing of 1972 when the B-52 had been shot down, Xuan said. Flowers lay at the front of a statue of clustered figures representing the thirty-or-so patients and staff killed by the bomb that was "mistakenly dropped" that holiday season, Xuan said, graciously granting the Americans the benefit of the doubt.

After a brief tour, the task force was taken to an abandoned villa on Hai Ba Trung Street to meet with Vietnamese officials. This villa had served as the U.S. Consulate in colonial times. After introductions around the table (even Mick was introduced as a reporter for Voice America, which solicited looks of disdain because V.O.A. was a thorn in the side of the Communists because its broadcasts could be heard in Vietnam), Damphier, who looked distinguished with his wavy silver hair and wire rim glasses, began the meeting by reading Article 8 of the Paris Peace Agreement signed in 1973, ending America's direct combat role in the war.

"The return of captured military personnel and foreign civilians shall be carried out simultaneously with troop withdrawals. The parties shall help each other to get information about those military personnel and foreign civilians of the parties missing in action, to determine the location and take care of the graves of the dead so as to facilitate the exhumation and repatriation of the remains."

"Yes," one of the Vietnamese said. "We understand this and we wish to cooperate fully."

"To start with," Damphier said, "an American Air Force fighter pilot was shot down near Nam Dinh south of Hanoi in 1969 in a dog fight with a MIG. His former wing man designated the area here on this map where he was last seen going down without deploying a parachute. We would like to search for remains there first. Can you provide us with transportation?"

"Of course," another of the Vietnamese said. "We were informed earlier that this was an area you would be interested in. It is case #369. You will be flown in a helicopter first thing in the morning, accompanied by Nguyen Phu Binh and Le Thanh Tau. A clearing has been made in the jungle near the suspected crash site where you will land."

In the morning Mick boarded the chopper along with the task force and the two Vietnamese. Damphier, being elderly, stayed behind in Hanoi to help coordinate other cases that would be undertaken after 369.

Mick never thought he'd be flying over North Vietnam. He had flown over South Vietnam many times, and he was always struck by its vast beauty, except in the areas that had been defoliated and bombed. And he had flown above the higher elevations of mountains which had remained untouched by the war. He had seen the waterfalls tumbling down through the jungle where huge, brightly-colored flowers grew. He had seen elephants meandering down a trail, trunk-to-tail.

It wasn't long before they set down in the clearing. Nearby The task force found a substantial hole in the ground nearby where the missing plane had possibly gone down. They began to excavate and sift through the soil with boxed screens, hoping to find teeth, bones, a belt buckle, dog tags, anything that would confirm the pilot's fate. Not a trace remained of a plane, which, had there been one, would most certainly have been salvaged by locals, and taken piece-by-piece to be sold in the nearest town as scrap.

Finally, miraculously, the task force found teeth. Were they Lt. Dan Kaslowski's? Time would tell. The teeth would be flown to a military-contracted forensic dentist in San Francisco for a positive I.D., which was probable. After all, who else's teeth would have been buried where Lt. Kaslowski's plane was thought to have gone down -- Amelia Earhart's?

Next case, Khe Sanh, to look for Rick Jenkin's brother-in-law, Major Rusty Dixon. They had flown there from Hanoi in an old U.S. C-123 cargo plane that had been captured during the fall of Saigon. Landing there brought back many memories to Mick, some harrowing. He had been to Khe Sanh to cover the siege in January of 1968 for Armed Forces Radio. He could see that the base had changed dramatically since then. Having stubbornly held out under a constant artillery, rocket and mortar barrage day after day for weeks, the Americans had dug in deep in underground bunkers, including the hospital, which was always filled to capacity. The airstrip had been littered on both sides by the wreckage of cargo planes that had been shot down coming in, or blasted once they had landed. Mick would have been on one that was shot down, but he missed the flight by ten minutes, so he came in on the next one that made it.

Now the base had been rebuilt above ground to accommodate the Vietnamese army and air force.

The task force was housed in barracks, and they ate in a chow hall -- Vietnamese fare; noodles and dog primarily, Nguyen Phu Binh informed them, causing Mick to skip the meat. He just couldn't reconcile eating Fido.

After lunch they set out for Hill 881, guided by a Vietnamese soldier who had fought there on the date Dixon had gone missing in '68. Binh recalled the intensity of the firefight, and how close the fighting had become. In the confusion, "...prisoners were taken by both sides," he said. "The Americans withdrew with theirs back to Khe Sanh, and we fled with ours into the jungle."

Jenkins didn't like hearing this -- the possibility that his brother-in-law was one of the soldiers that the enemy had captured. They searched for remains anyway just for the chance of turning up something -- anything. Maybe a dog tag had survived the elements: more likely, though, it would be bone or tooth -- if he had been killed there, or wounded and left to die -- but after a week of searching, the task force came up empty-handed.

The next case, 251, would take the task force even farther south to Dak To in the Central Highlands, home territory of the renowned Montagnards. First though, they'd fly to Da Nang in the 123 to pick up a new member of the task force, a former Green Beret, Tom Waterman. Then they'd fly on to Dak To in a Soviet-built helicopter that was the equivalent of an American Chinook chopper that could accommodate cargo as large as Jeeps and about twenty passengers. The task force consisted of seven now, with the addition of Waterman. Also joining them at Da Nang was Nguyen Xuan, who had infiltrated the South from the North on the Ho Chi Minh Trail in 1974. His familiarity with the Trail would be invaluable in guiding the task force to where they needed to go to resolve case 251.

After a relatively short trip from Da Nang, they set down at Dak To, which had been the scene of a horrific battle between American forces and the North Vietnamese in 1967. On the surrounding hilltops, craters from the bombing and mortars, and the scraggly remnants of trees, remained as reminders of the battle. Casualties had been high on both sides, but the Americans prevailed.

From Dak To they took an old Vietnamese troop truck thirty miles up old French Route 14 to Dak Pek where Waterman had served while living with the Montagnard tribe, the Jeh. He still wore the round brass bracelets the chief had given him as a token of friendship.

"This entire area is where the Ho Chi Minh Trail spilled out of Laos and Cambodia into Nam," he pointed out. "The jungle around here was crawling with North Vietnamese and Viet Cong. Dak Pek was established by the American Special Forces to protect the surrounding Montagnard villages from the infiltrating Communists. There, on the hill is the village of Dak Jel Kong. It's a Jeh tribe. I may still know some of the inhabitants. If so, it would be a good launching point for our mission. It's about 50 miles from the Cambodian border, about a four day hike, and another ten miles to Hill 61 where the LURPS were last accounted for."

Waterman passed around a map showing the hill circled in red, with a line drawn from it to Dak Pek.

"That's as the crow flies, but in reality we'll be winding around up and down mountains and across streams following the old Ho Chi Minh Trail, which actually isn't just a trail, but an intertwining network of roads, dirt paths and arteries. It may not be very passable anymore, since it hasn't been used for more than two years. The jungle takes over fast around here with all the rain and tropical heat. Park the truck, we'll walk up to the village from here."

Halfway up the hill, the task force was met by a handful of Jeh tribesmen wearing loin cloths and old short-sleeved army fatigue shirts left over from the Green Beret days, according to the insignias. Their earlobes were adorned with ivory plugs, and their upper front teeth were filed down to the gums, apparently a look considered attractive among the Jehs.

Waterman, who still sported a military-style haircut that served to highlight his lean, tan, angular face and piercing blue eyes, smiled at them broadly and he held up his arm and jingled his bracelets. The lead tribesman, an older man with a multitude of bracelets on his arms, responded in kind, chuckling and he nodded several times indicating he recognized Waterman, and they embraced. They said something to each other in Jeh, and the leader guided his old friend into the village and the others followed.

They went to a long, thatched-roof house that was built on poles.

"This is a communal house," Waterman, whose height forced him to stoop when he stood in the doorway, said to the others. "A *marao* where visitors are welcomed. They will feed us, and afterwards we'll be expected to drink rice wine. If you refuse to drink the wine with the chief, it means he will die."

The chief understood some English and he laughed and nodded at what Waterman said.

That was good enough for Mick. He sure as hell didn't want the chief to die, but first they'd eat. Bare-breasted women in wrap-around skirts brought a huge wooden platter of steaming food, and smaller plates for the men of the tribe and the task force, along with bamboo twigs for chop sticks.

"It's a kind of a stew of roasted monkey smothered in vegetables," Waterman said, "and possibly some rat, bat and lizard mixed in."

Mick ate without hesitation. He was still hungry after six months of near starvation in Cambodia.

After every morsel of food was devoured, the women took the platter and plates away and lit torches to help the men see, and the tribesmen lit pipes and two of them carried in a vat of rice wine and ladled it into wooden cups for everyone.

Soon the tribesmen began to converse in Jeh, but they directed their conversation to Waterman knowing that what they talked about needed to be translated for the benefit of their visitors.

"They talk of the spirits of the Yang and the Kanam, and the significance of the rainbow that shone on our arrival. The Yang rule the sky, the earth, the mountains and the rivers. They are respected, and considered to be relatively good spirits. They can control the

Kanam, who are evil ancestor spirits that roam the forests, demanding appeasement and bringing untold misfortune to the lives of men."

Shadows of the men danced on the walls as the wind blew the flames of the torches.

"The chief is concerned that the rainbow that appeared upon our arrival is the work of the Kanam. The Jeh believe that an evil spirit lives at the end of the rainbow," Waterman related. "It sucks up water from the rivers and gives it to the spirits of those who have died unnatural deaths, like the many Montagnards who have died in war. These evil spirts wander in the forest and bring all kinds of hardships. Rainbows of the Kanam are things to be dreaded, not welcomed, so tomorrow the tribe will sacrifice a pig to the good spirit Yang so it will ward of any misfortune brought on by the Kanam-produced rainbow, which could endanger us on our journey to Hill 61."

Waterman had told the chief about the task force's mission. The Jeh were familiar with the terrain they'd be traversing. They would lead the task force to the border with Cambodia along the Ho Chi Minh Trail, then verbally direct them to the mountains where Hill 61 sat in Cambodia. Waterman had shown the chief the hill circled on the map and he roughly recognized its location.

"We'll leave tomorrow after the pig has been sacrificed and consumed," Waterman said, having taken over the lead of the task force, although Nguyen Xuan would be instrumental in guiding them on the old Trail.

"That'll give us plenty of food in the belly for the beginning of our trip. Meanwhile, drink and be merry, the chief expects the vat to be emptied tonight."

And Mick did his best to accommodate the chief. He was no stranger to rice wine. He had consumed it plentifully with a Vietnamese friend in Saigon where he lived most of the time during the war.

Feeling playful, Mick turned on his tape recorder and put the microphone to the mouths of the tribesmen who were telling stories, then he played it back. They were utterly amused to hear their own voices coming from the little box. One of them, obviously high on wine sang a song into the microphone while playing a three-string dulcimer-like instrument. It became quite a party with much laughter and music, but the pungent smell of the smoke of whatever the Jeh had in their pipes, and the potent wine got the best of Mick, and he passed out where he sat on the hard, woven bamboo floor. While he was asleep, one of the tribesmen slipped two brass bracelets onto his arm. He was surprised to discover them in the morning when he awoke to a smiling Jeh woman bending over him with a pipe which she offered to him to smoke.

"It's their cure for hangovers, and it will give you an appetite for the sacrificed pig," Waterman, who was standing nearby, said.

Mick thought, "...hum, must be like marijuana," the only cure for a hangover he had ever known, and it made him eat like a pig.

Chapter 15

With bellies full and the curse of the rainbow lifted, the task force set out on their mission to Cambodia, with two Jeh tribesmen and Nguyen Xuan. Xuan had changed from his nice street clothes and sandals to boots and fatigues, looking every bit the North Vietnamese soldier he'd been in the American war years. He didn't appear to have aged much. He had been very young as a soldier, as many of them were; some not much older than fifteen, like their Viet Cong counterparts.

They started off on a path that gradually became one of the many tentacles of the Ho Chi Minh Trail, which spread out like a river delta from Cambodia into Vietnam. Finally, after walking on the narrow path through tall grass, scrub brush and bamboo, they hit the main trail that went through thick jungle.

They traveled relatively light, packing hammocks, mosquito nets and packets of freeze-dried food that required water to make them edible. The heaviest things they carried were shovels and picks, and canteens of water. The dirt-sifting screen boxes which two of the task force carried, were cumbersome but light. Mick carried the tape recorder, slung over one shoulder and beneath the other, and tapes in the big leg pockets of his camouflage army fatigue pants.

The Jeh cleared the way with a homemade machete-like tool called a *mak*. They chopped vines and thick foliage, and with the tool they deftly beheaded a rat which they put in a canvas satchel to be saved for a meal later. They had also packed sacks of rice. Mick wondered how they would cook it without a pot.

Suddenly a small, bright green snake dropped from the trees and one of the Jeh hacked it in half with his *mak*. Then he clamped his arm with his fingers and thumb simulating a snake bite, and he snapped his fingers, rolled back his eyes and swooned, feigning quick death.

As they moved along Mick saw little monkeys swinging high up in the trees, chattering incessantly at the intruders. He found it difficult to think about having eaten one of thesw playful, child-like creatures the night before. He reluctantly admitted though, that it had tasted good, being the only meat he'd had for six months, except for the bit of lizard he ate in the cellar of the Hotel Angkor with Lovea.

While walking along he thought of Lovea. Had she been able to organize a counterinsurgency after all, with the help of Colonel Yon and the CIA?

After ten miles or so of going up and down and around mountains through jungle, they stopped to camp for the night. They strung their hammocks in the trees and draped them with mosquito nets. The Jeh would sleep on the ground on broad leaf palms they cut down. Waterman explained they were impervious to mosquitoes because they rubbed tobacco on their skin -- a natural repellent.

While the task force ate from the pouches of freeze-dried food with which they mixed water, the Jeh built a fire of dead wood, and they answered Mick's question about how they'd cook the rice. They chopped off the partitioned hollow section of a bamboo tube, cut a hole in the top and poured the rice with water in, and rested the tube on rocks on either side of the fire, and it boiled. They then hacked off one end of the tube and viola -- cooked rice, which they ate with the rat they had killed and roasted.

After everyone had eaten they sat around the fire. It had gotten so dark that nothing could be seen beyond the glow of the flames. Neither moon nor stars were visible above the dense tree canopy.

Mick asked Xuan what it had been like on the Ho chi Minh Trail during the war. Xuan had plenty to say.

"It was difficult marching under the weight of our packs. In the heat and humidity we were forced to stop often to rest and catch our breath. At night, utterly exhausted, we'd hang our hammocks and mosquito nets from the trees and fall asleep. At times we would search far from the trail for a waterfall or spring where we could drink and fill our canteens. We built fires with green bamboo to send smoke up into the trees to bring down bats to eat. There are tigers and leopards here in the jungle; they attack stragglers and people who have become separated, so beware," Xuan warned. "We climbed mountain faces of over a thousand meters, and from the summit a spectacle of splendor and magnificence lay before us. It was like a countryside of fairy tales, but when the American bombers came, the B-52s, it became a land of nightmares. Many were killed, but we marched on. We had faith in our struggle, in our leaders and in our country to endure the suffering and pain. We had faith that someday our country would be reunited as it is today after the great victory."

With Xuan's last resounding word, came silence around the fire. He was the only one there who had been victorious, and they couldn't begrudge him that. He and his people had endured much during the war to make Ho Chi Minh's dream of a united Vietnam come true. Although there were many in the South who were opposed to a Communist take over, unfortunately the Americans didn't keep up with the opposition long enough. They left in disgrace in '73.

Mick found his way through the dark to his hammock where he was kept awake for a while by the cacophonous night sounds of the jungle which gradually subsided into one in particular that resembled that of a mourning dove cooing -- a peaceful sound that lulled him to sleep.

Chapter 16

After two more nights and three days on the Trail the Jeh informed the task force that they had reached Cambodia, so they turned back. Xuan would lead the way now to Hill 61. The Jeh kindly left him the *mak*, as they had cleared enough of the Trail that far to return on it.

They set up camp early that day. The terrain had been especially rugged and they needed the rest.

While Mick lay in his hammock he heard what sounded like a waterfall in the distance. It would make good background sound for one of his reports, he thought. He had already recorded the sounds of the jungle at night.

He wandered off toward the sound of the rushing water. The jungle was thick but passable enough. After a while, perhaps an hour, he came to a narrow river at the foot of the waterfall. It was high and great volumes of water roared over the edge. He stepped down the bank of the river to get a little closer and he slipped, and his ankle became wedged between two boulders. He struggled to get loose, but he couldn't. He tried to pull his foot out of his boot, but it was just too tight and he couldn't reach the laces to loosen them because of the way his foot was caught. He called for help, but his cries were drowned out by the roar of the falling water pouring into the river. He could only hope that the others would look for him in the direction in which he'd gone, but they'd have to hurry. It was nearly dark and he had been trapped for nearly two hours.

He was in such a position that he couldn't sit down; his legs grew weary and his ankle throbbed with pain. Soon mosquitoes began to bite his face, neck, arms and hands. He wanted to scream, but instead he prayed -- which he hadn't done in some time, but he hadn't forgotten how. In essence, he begged his higher power to somehow set him free.

Night fell and it was pitch dark until the moon drifted over the falls and cast light on the banks of the narrow river. Mick thought he saw something moving in the shadows of a thicket of bamboo on the opposite bank, which was only a stone's throw away. He watched intently, wondering what it might be. Then he saw two greenish-yellow eyes that seemed to be peering at him. They belonged to a big black cat whose shiny fur shone in the moonlight.

Mick held his breath to a trickle and he stayed perfectly still. He remembered what Xuan had said about those who wandered off of the trail being vulnerable to tiger and panther attacks.

The cat crept closer to the water, and his eyes still appeared to be focused on Mick. Was he coming across?

Mick very slowly unslung his tape recorder; he'd use it as a weapon if he had to fend off the cat. But then it stopped at the water's edge and drank. It must not have been hungry enough to come after Mick. Finally it turned away and Mick was able to breathe again.

Being forced to stand up he couldn't sleep; besides, the pain in his leg and the mosquitoes wouldn't allow it. He'd have to stay that way until morning when the task force would surely come looking for him. However, he was able to put some weight on his hands which relieved some of the pressure on his legs that quivered from fatigue.

Even if they found him, though, would they be able to free him? They had a *mak* – they could cut off his leg. Mick was serious. That might be the only option to staying there forever. No way could those men move the boulders the size of those between which he was trapped.

Morning finally came with the hope of the task force finding him. But by the time the sun was straight up in the sky, they hadn't. The sun beat down on him mercilessly. The humidity drained him dry. He had a little water left in his canteen. He drank of it frugally, only to forestall the inevitability of dying of thirst -- or of being eaten alive by that cat who had come to the river to drink the night before.

After the sun went down and the moon reappeared above the falls the cat came back, and again it seemed disinterested in Mick. It must have come to drink with a full belly. What he wouldn't give to have a full belly. He remembered how good the pig that the Jeh had sacrificed to Kaman to ward off the evil spirits of the rainbow had tasted. So this is where the curse of that rainbow had led him. The sacrifice had gone for naught.

He watched the cat, envious of its freedom. Mick felt like a tree rooted between the boulders. If only he could walk again. It would be another sleepless night, although his legs had already gone to sleep from lack of use. He massaged, them trying to get the circulation back, but it only brought back the pain in his ankle which was excruciating -- like it was being crushed. In essence it was. He began to faint, and he fell forward into a position he hadn't been able to manage before, and his suddenly his ankle popped free, and he tumbled head over heels down the bank to the edge of the river. His prayer had been answered. He gingerly got to his feet and tried to walk but his legs were like jelly. He sat down and took off his boot and sock and examined his ankle. It was very sore, badly bruised and abraded, but it didn't seem to be broken. He tested it again and he was able to put some weight on it -- but of course he wouldn't go anywhere that night. He was too elated to sleep, so he just lay back and looked at the stars and thanked his higher power for setting him free.

At first light, after refilling his canteen, he limped back toward the trail he thought he had taken. After about two hours of fighting through the jungle he did arrive at a trail, but he wasn't sure it was the one he had been on before with the task force. There was no sign that foliage had been cut to make a path with the *mak*. This trail was fairly overgrown, but passable. Being somewhat disoriented, though, he wasn't sure about which direction to go, and it was difficult to see where the sun was because of the triple canopy of trees.

Mick limped along the path as it went higher and higher. He still couldn't see where the sun rose and set because of the mountain mist. If he got to the summit perhaps he'd be able to tell, if the sun peeked above the mist.

He was awfully hungry. He looked about for a particular green plant whose root was similar to a potato. He had learned about them on his way to Nam when he was required to stop in the Phillippines for jungle survival school. Because he would be flying a lot, he needed to know how to survive off the land if he were shot down. Luckily he found a couple of the plants, and when he came to a stream that poured into a placid pool before it cascaded into rapids further down, he saw the silvery flash of fish in the pool. As a youth he had learned from a nature boy how to catch fish with his bare hands. He took off his boots and socks, cuffed his pants legs and slowly waded in. After several tries he caught one. But he also came out of the pool with leeches all over his legs. After tearing them off, which was like ripping tape from his skin, he ate the fish raw, desperate for protein. The jungle potatoes provided carbohydrates. He sat for a while waiting for the nutrition to take effect, then he moved on. After about two miles he happened upon a gruesome scene – a circle of six skeletons with rusting GI dog tags around their necks. He was able to determine that they belonged to U.S. Marines. They must have been the LURPS who went missing in '72 -- the ones the task force was looking for. Was this Hill 61? If so, the task force had missed it. How would he be able to recover the remains without them? He sure as hell couldn't carry six skeletons back to Nam -- but then again, neither could they. They were expecting to find, if anything, only teeth, bone fragments and dog tags, not complete skeletons. Practicality dictated that teeth be extracted from the skulls; with these, and the dog tags a positive I.D. could be made, which would qualify the remains for repatriation, and symbolic burials could take place back in the World.

Mick concluded that he could put a tooth with the corresponding dog tag in each of his six pockets and take those back to Nam if he could find the way. But weren't there supposed to have been seven on this patrol? Someone was missing.

Mick went around the circle reading the dog tag names. In the process he discovered a large combat knife in the skeletal hand of Lance Corporal Raymond Bodden. He used it to pry teeth from the skulls, then he collected the dog tags and put each in separate pockets.

And with the knife he was able to cut vines to make a hammock. Until now he had been sleeping on the ground where he was bitten badly by ants.

He intertwined the vines that he'd cut, making a sturdy hammock in which he lay, and being very tired he drifted off to sleep immediately. After a while he was awakened by what he thought were voices coming from the valley below. Had the task force finally arrived? If so, they had set up camp. He smelled smoke. He started to head down to the valley when he suddenly realized the voices he heard weren't speaking English. With his knife in hand he crept closer to investigate, choosing each step carefully so as not to make noise. His Montagnard bracelets clinked slightly so he separated them, one on each arm.

He then came to a ridge that overlooked an encampment on the other side of a substantial stream, and he was taken aback by what he saw – Khmer Rouge. They wore the tell-tale black uniforms, and red and white checkered scarfs. He counted ten of them, and an eleventh that sat with his back against a tree, but he wasn't a Cambodian. He was a bearded white man. One of the soldiers brought him a bowl, and he ate from it with his fingers. When the soldier came back for the bowl, he bound the man's hands with twine behind the tree. He was obviously a prisoner. Could this be Hubbard, the seventh LURP? If so, he had been a prisoner for some time.

Mick had a knife. He could sneak up and cut him loose as soon as it got dark. But did he have the balls to try it? If he were caught he'd be as good as dead, or a prisoner himself. It would be dangerous coming down off the ridge in total darkness, then going through the stream without making a splash. He lay low, trying to muster up enough courage to do it. If he acted at all, he'd wait for the soldiers to turn in, and for the fire to die down. When it did he crawled down from the ridge through the undergrowth like a snake slithering through a thicket of bamboo until he came to the stream. The encampment was situated above the stream and about 30 yards back from it. Mick would have to crawl up the embankment and another 10 yards to reach the prisoner.

He crouched down and waded through the stream very quietly. He crawled the ten yards up behind the man who wasn't aware of Mick's presence until he tapped his arm. The man jumped and Mick put his finger to his lips to tell him to be quiet, but he responded in a whisper telling Mick his name was Hubbard and he was an American Marine, if Mick was a commando looking specifically for him. Mick cut him loose. As they descended into the stream one of the soldiers spotted them and he shouted and fired his gun. As he chased after them other soldiers followed in quick succesion, and Mick and Hubbard continued running through the shallow stream. It would be faster than trying to run up the hill through the dense underbrush, but the stones in the stream proved to be very slippery and Mick fell hitting his head on one, and it knocked him half-conscious momentarily, just long enough for the soldiers to overtake him. One of them pounced on Mick's back and choked him from behind with his rifle, and they quickly recaptured Hubbard who had tried to make a break for it up the hill, but got hung up in the bamboo. The soldiers marched Mick and Hubbard back to the encampment at the ends of the their rifle barrels, then they knocked them face down and bound their hands behind them with twine, so tightly that it cut into Mick's wrists. One of the soldiers slapped him hard on the back of his head.

"You American commando?" he demanded to know.

"You Americn Commando?" he slapped Mick again.

"No, Voice of America, reporter, *bao chi*," Mick said using the Vietnamese words for reporter, thinking the soldier, although Cambodian, might understand. He understood all right.

"Voice of America," he shouted with disdain, then he spit on Mick. "Voice of America say very bad things about Khmer Rouge, Pol Pot," the soldier growled in broken English.

The soldier pressed his foot down hard on the back of Mick's neck. "What you say now, Voice of America?"

Mick didn't say anything. The soldier yanked him to his feet and pushed him along with his rifle to a tree where he undid his wrists and retied them around the trunk and bound his ankles with the twine.

"You will go nowhere tonight until we march tomorrow," the soldier, who appeared to be the leader, said, and he bound Hubbard to another tree.

"And you will be punished for trying to escape. No rice for you two days," he said to Hubbard.

Hubbard looked gaunt enough, Mick thought, and he could tell by the way he had run that he didn't have much strength. Neither did

Mick. He had been eating sparingly. Maybe they'd give him rice in the morning.

It got cool at night in the mountains and Mick was wet from being in the stream. The coolness didn't deter the mosquitos though. They bit him all over and buzzed around his ears keeping him awake all night, but the soldiers slept, apparently unconcerned about any attempt by their prisoners to escape.

At dawn's first light the soldiers cut Mick and Hubbard loose. They gave Mick a skimpy bowl of rice.

"Hurry, eat. We march soon," the leader of the soldiers ordered.

"The rice was sticky and easy to eat with fingers. Mick gobbled it down, then the soldiers formed a line, with the first two wielding machetes, and they marched with Mick and Hubbard in the middle, down a wide beaten path, that, because it was so worn and passable, Mick assumed to be an artery of the greater Ho Chi Minh Trail. They marched for three days. Each night they stopped to camp and the two prisoners were tied to trees after being fed rice. They were given a bowl in the morning and one in the evening, and Hubbard finally got some.

When the soldiers were a safe distance away, Hubbard whispered to Mick that the they were looking for Vietnamese invaders who had begun forays into Cambodia in preparation, they thougt, for an all-out invasion. "They've had contact before -- short firefights. The Khmer Rouge lost two in the last one, but they've held their own for the most part, chasing the Vietnamese off each time.

"Where in the hell did you come from anyway?" Hubbard asked.

Mick explained that he had been with a task force searching for lost LURPS, before he got separated from the others. "Were you one of them? I found the remains of six not far from where we tried to escape."

"They're dead huh? I figured as much. We were overrun."

"How long have you been held captive?" Mick asked.

"I don't know, I've lost track of time." Hubbard's hollow gray eyes were downcast.

"You went missing in '73, this is '77"

"That long, huh?" He shook his head.

"Time flies when you're having fun." He managed a slight smile.

"Ever try to escape, before I came along?" Mick asked.

"Twice, but each time I was too weak to get very far. They keep me malnnourished. As a result I've got scurvy, and my teeth are falling out. Shhh, here they come."

"What you talk about? Escape?" the leader asked as he put the barrel of his rifle between Mick's eyes and pushed his head back hard against the tree.

"Try to escape, Voice of America? This time we shoot!"

Mick had no intention of escaping, just yet. They were watching him too closely. Sooner or later though, they'd let their guard down. They were inclined to do so at night, but that's when they tied him up, tightly, with the twine that cut into his wrists. The slightest movement caused intense, burning pain, so it was difficult to maneuver his hands around for his fingers to feel the knot. If he did, then perhaps he could work it loose. He tried, and one of the soldiers saw him struggling and he went behind the tree and kicked his hands and then he tied the knot even tighter and Mick's hands went numb, eliminating the pain, and he slumped off to sleep. In the morning the soldiers freed Hubbard and him from their trees, and they marched on again father down the trail. Through the canopy Mick saw the sun, and judging from its position they were heading west deeper into Cambodia away from the border as if they were shying away from any more confrontations with the Vietnamese. But there was another enemy they were concerned about, according to what Hubbard had managed to tell Mick while the soldiers slept.

"They think there's a group of Cambodian counterinsurgents stalking them. That's what they've been jabbering about all day. They are very nervous."

"How do they know? I mean how do they know they're not Vietnamese?

"Because one of their scouts reported catching a fleeting glimpse of one of them and the camouflage uniform was not that of the Vietnamese army, but similar in style to those of the fledgling People's Republican Army, known as the War Wolves, who have been responsible for ambushing small isolated groups of Khmer Rouge like this one.

Adding insult to injury the War Wolves are thought to be led by a woman."

As if with a lightning bolt Mick was struck by this revelation. Could the War Wolves be Lovea's counterinsurgents? They must be; after all, how many Cambodian women would have the moxie to attack the Khmer Rouge? She was determined all right, to avenge her mother's cold blooded murder, and the cold blooded murder of millions of Cambodians by Pol Pot and his Khmer Rouge.

"Why do they seem so much more concerned about the People's Republican Army than the Vietnamese?"

"Because the PRA take no prisoners, one of the soldiers told me," Hubbard said. "They attack at night under a full moon and they howl. That's their battle cry, to terrorize their enemy. That's why they're called the War Wolves by the Khmer Rouge."

Chapter 17

A full moon illuminated the encampment of the Khmer Rouge, who had discovered a vat of rice wine in a deserted rice farmer's house. They were drinking it freely with wild abandonment, laughing and singing, unaware that they were being watched through the surrounding jungle. This was careless behavior for any army that was being stalked by Vietnamese and Cambodian counterinsurgents alike. They would be easy prey if drunk. And the War Wolves showed no mercy when they attacked, slashing through the trees with finely-honed machetes. In a flash, all the Khmer Rouge lay dead – decapitated. They'd be found that way by the next ones who came along who'd know that the War Wolves had struck again, as they were known to use machetes in sneak attacks instead of noisy rifles and grenades so as not to alert any other Khmer Rouge who might be in the vicinity.

After the attack the War Wolves went back to their sanctuary in Ankgor Wat where they dispersed temporarily. All went their separate ways in the labyrinth of passageways that led to and from countless edifices, pavilions and chambers where they slept separately to avoid being attacked en masse, although all combatants seemed to have agreed, yes, even the Khmer Rouge, that the temple complex was immune from major battles, but pock marks from bullets were visible throughout, most likely the result of the random vandalism of drunken soldiers from all factions.

The War Wolves would regroup the following day to eat and plan their next mission. They always planned their missions around the waxing and waning of the full moon using its light three nights before and three nights after it was full. On this night, the second night of waning, it shone through the moving clouds on the long, mold-splotched sandstone wall of bas-relief across from an alcove where

Lovea had fashioned a thick bed of palm leaves. She had a clear view of the moonlit wall that depicted (as she knew from visits there with her father) the Hindu creation myth known as "The Churning of the Sea of Milk," where multitudes of fish and reptiles swirl about in the seminal fluid from which springs the ambrosia of immortality. And above it all, riding a giant tortoise, is Brahma, the lotus-bearing Hindu god of creation, surrounded by celestial maidens who serve as messengers between lesser gods and humans born of the sea.

Moonlight flickered through the passing clouds like a strobe light, making the phantasmagoria of Khmer lore appear to be moving like a motion picture, and Lovea lay awake for much of the night mesmerized by the sight.

In the morning, after a some sleep, she bathed in the moat, while washing the blood-stained clothes she had worn in the attack on the drunken Khmer Rouge. She then donned the fresh ones she had washed the day before. Then she met with others in the middle of the complex around a fire on which they boiled rice and ate figs and bananas.

While eating, Lovea could faintly see in the distance the DC-3 in which she, Sabay, Lam Linh, Tran Van and Mick had been shot down. They had escaped certain death by splash-landing in a rice paddy, but Sabay died from a gunshot wound he'd sustained when the Khmer Rouge fired on the plane as they took off from the airport at Phnom Penh.

Lovea wondered if she would ever see the others again. She missed Mick especially. They had bonded in the wine cellar of the Hotel Angkor where she was hiding from the Khmer Rouge -- but not romantically. Not that she was adverse to it, but the circumstances were hardly conducive to romance. There were rats and lizards in the dank cellar, and the mattress on which she slept musty and damp. No place to make love, for sure.

Lovea was awakened from her daydream by the return of a War Wolves scout who reported the enemy were in control of the little nearby provincial capital of Siem Reap, where they were holed up in the old Grand Hotel built in the 1960s by the French to accommodate tourists to the Angkor temples.

To attack them late at night as they slept, the War Wolves would have to go south through three and a half miles of dense forest to reach Siem Reap under a waning moon on the third night past full. There was just enough light by which to see, and conversely, by which to be seen, if enemy sentries were posted outside the town, but the War Wolves encountered none. When they arrived at the northern edge of the town they encircled it intending to meet in the center of town at the hotel -- at midnight. They synchronized their watches before spreading out. At midnight, as a unit, they slipped into the hotel. A guard stood in the lobby with his back to the door. Colonel Yon, who despite being middle-aged, was a tenacious warrior. He sneaked up behind the Khmer Rouge guard and cut his throat as the others quietly streamed up the stairs and went room-to-room with pistols and daggers in hand, their weapons of choice instead of rifles which would be cumbersome to maneuver in hand-to-hand combat in close quarters. They caught their enemy by surprise in the first three rooms, but then they were detected and a running gun battle ensued throughout the hotel, reminiscent of the fighting in the U.S. Embassy in Saigon during the Tet offensive of '68.

Putting her French martial art kick-boxing skills, called savate to good use with sweeping high kicks, Lovea battled her way from room to room, shooting her pistol and wielding her dagger. She killed four single-handedly before being hit in the head by the butt of a rifle, sending her head over heels down the stairs, and she found herself lying half-conscious on her back looking up at a Khmer Rouge who put the barrel of his rifle between her eyes, but before he pulled the trigger Ing Pech shot him. Ing took special pleasure in it. At Tuol Sleng he had witnessed many prisoners with the barrels of AK-47s being pointed between their eyes at point-blank range and the trigger was usually pulled without his being able to do anything about it. As a former teacher of English he recalled the Shakespearian quote, "Revenge tastes sweetest when served up cold." He looked down at the dead Khmer Rouge and smiled. There was vengeance in his heart.

All in all 15 of the enemy were slain, while only five War Wolves were wounded. The lightning-quick battle lasted a mere 20 minutes, and the War Wolves were able to withdraw before more Khmer Rouge arrived on the scene.

In the meantime, the slain Khmer Rouge got their just desserts. When word got out that several had been killed in the hotel, some of the citizens of Siem Reap dragged the bodies to the outskirts of town where they piled them in an open grave as the Khmer Rouge had done to many of them.

One of the wounded Wolves, was Colonel Yon. At first it was thought that the bullet, which had entered his lower back and exited his side, had missed vital organs, but he began to piss blood profusely. A War Wolf who had been a medic in Lon Nol's army attended to him religiously, literally. He said Buddhist prayers over him night and day. That was all he could do -- the Colonel died. Lovea wept openly. He had been the patriarch of the People's Republican Army – a founding father. Using a folding shovel, they buried him in a glade of rhododendron.

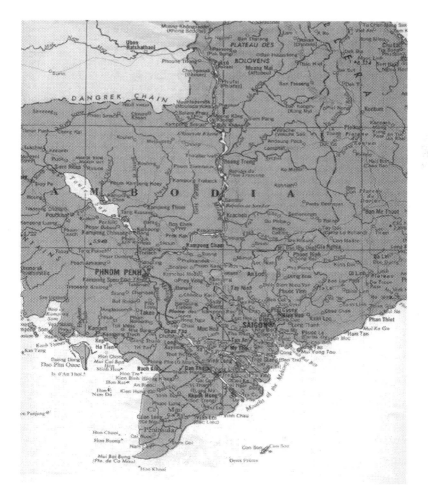

Chapter 18

Despite the loss of Colonel Yon, the morale of the War Wolves remained high for a while as a result of their triumphs over the enemy in northwest Cambodia, so they boldly ventured into northeast Cambodia, where the Khmer Rouge had originated when they were allies of the Viet Cong and the North Vietnamese Army in the days of Communist sympathizer Prince Sihanouk -- before Lon Nol and Pol Pot. It was thought by Lovea that if the War Wolves could make inroads into enemy strongholds the word would get out to enemy forces in Phnom Penh that there was trouble on the eastern front. This, along with the fact that skirmishes were reported to have taken place along the border between Khmer Rouge and the Vietnamese army, would shake Pol Pot's confidence in being able to rule the country uncontested.

The War Wolves were forced to cross several small rivers on rafts they built of bamboo, light enough for four to carry between the rivers until they came to the mighty Mekong. There were no villages between Angkor Wat and Phum Siembauk on the western bank of the Mekong, so they had not encountered Khmer Rouge for the entire 130 miles, which took them ten days. They ate well, feasting on fish along the way. They needed the strength to carry the rafts, but most of all they needed it to battle the enemy who occupied Phum Siembauk. This time they used all the weapons at their disposal -- M-16s and grenade launchers provided by the U.S. Air Force security police at Udorn Air Base in Thailand, through the CIA. But the War Wolves had not previously engaged in open warfare in the light of day. They were guerrilla fighters who specialized in surprise attacks at night, so when they encountered the enemy in the streets of the town at high noon they sustained heavy casualties, and they were forced to retreat to the waterfront where they confiscated sampans left behind by the town's fishermen who had long been relocated to collective farms to grow rice. They crossed the Mekong with bullets flying all around them. They left five dead behind. On the opposite shore they regrouped and took inventory on their ammunition supply which was running low. All they had left were bandoliers of M-16 rifle and .45 pistol magazines.

To survive, and to conserve ammo, they'd have to revert back to ambushing the enemy on patrol in between the towns at night. No more open warfare in the streets in broad daylight. They'd utilize guerrilla tactics such as those once employed by the Viet Minh/Viet Cong in South Vietnam against the French and Americans.

On the trails that they observed were being used by the Khmer Rouge, they dug pits and planted punji stakes in them and covered the pits with brush for unsuspecting enemy to step into. They carefully looped twine around the stems of the huge pinata-like hives of very ill-tempered killer bees who were known to attack in swarms at the slightest provocation, and strung the twine across the trail. It worked to perfection one night when an enemy patrol came through and the point man tripped the twine. The bees attacked, sending the patrol screaming and scrambling down the trail, giving the War Wolves something to laugh at for a change, on the long, arduous journey that had recently dampened their morale, particularly since the death of Colonel Yon and the beating they took at Phum Siembauk.

They continued tracking northeast toward -- according to their maps -- the confluence of the Se San and Srepak Rivers near where Highway 19 crossed over the Srepak on a bridge. If they followed the highway far enough east it would take them to the isolated town of Andaung Pech, where a returning scout reported seeing armed guards forcing people to labor on a rubber tree plantation. At night, he said, they were being herded into dark, elevated long houses. The guards were housed in a separate one that had electricity. Their next mission would be to liberated the enslaved.

Two miles from the town they sent the scout out again to see what kind of defense was set up at the camp. He saw that there was a well-armed guard at each end of the three long houses, but oddly enough none at the one that housed the soldiers, of which there were about twenty as far as the scout could tell. To liberate the workers would require getting the drop on the guards then arming two workers in each long house with the captured weapons which would give the War Wolves a slight advantage in numbers when it came to attacking the guards' house.

The plan was to entice the three guards at the ends of the long houses nearest the rubber trees into the trees, which the War Wolves had climbed. To do this, they made noises like wild pigs grunting. A pig would provide abundant meat to go with the guards' mundane, and less than nutritious diet of rice and bananas and an occasional scrawny bat or rat.

Tempted, the guards left their posts and came into the trees, and the War Wolves literally got the drop on them by jumping down onto their backs and strangling them with the trademark red and white scarves they wore around their necks. They then entered the long houses and awoke the workers, quietly explaining what was going on, and offered the rifles of the guards they'd overcome to anyone interested in taking them. After overcoming the guards at the other ends of the long houses by strangling them too, they armed three more workers with the captured weapons and encircled the guards' house and called out, and when the guards came running out, they were gunned down one after another.

Again the dead guards were disposed of in a mass open grave, and the liberated workers returned to their homes in nearby Andaung Pech where most had been merchants who sold their wares in roadside stalls along the once-busy Highway 19 -- the only highway in the northeast quadrant of Cambodia between the major Mekong River town of Stoeng Treng and Pleiku in the Central Highlands of Vietnam. The Vietnamese were using it to launch incursions into Cambodia, but it was a two-way street. The Khmer Rouge launched incursions on the highway into Vietnam, and the opposing forces clashed. From a lofty perch on a jungle-covered ridge above the highway, the War Wolves watched them battle. The Vietnamese got the upper hand and sent the Khmer Rouge scrambling north toward the Se San River. With the Khmer Rouge in retreat, the Vietnamese moved farther west into Cambodia on Highway 19. The War Wolves stood down and planned their next mission, which would entail pursuing the enemy. They were on the run and the War Wolves were intent on tracking them down. They'd avenge Colonel Yon.

Chapter 19

With each passing night toward a waxing moon, the Khmer Rouge became more tense with the prospect of being attacked by the PRA when the moon became full. It made Mick more tense too. What would happen to him and Hubbard when the bullets started flying? Tied to trees they were defenseless. But if the PRA overwhelmed the Khmer Rouge and they survived the shooting, then they'd be set free. Then they'd follow the Trail, or an artery thereof, back to Vietnam.

How ironic that Mick would view Vietnam as a safe haven -- and it was, compared to bloody Cambodia, although the Vietnamese were responsible for some of the bloodletting in attacking the Khmer Rouge. Ironic too, considering they had been allies during Vietnam's war with America.

First the War Wolves attacked with grenades. Shrapnel ripped off chunks of tree above Mick's head. Then came the small arms fire. Streams of tracer bullets, like deadly laser beams, streaked through the encampment, electrifying the air. Mick's hair stood on end as the bullets zipped past his ears. With his hands tied behind him around the tree he slid down as far as he could, legs extended, but his head and shoulders and chest remained exposed.

The Khmer Rouge returned fire, launching grenades of their own, and the firefight raged on for twenty minutes or so, until the attackers came charging out of the jungle, howling. A couple of them were killed, shot at close range, but the others quickly overwhelmed the outnumbered Khmer Rouge. And leading the charge was a woman who Mick recognized immediately as Lovea, though they were some distance apart. Her gleaming hematite eyes reflected the light of the bright full moon. She rushed into the encampment and high-kicked a defender in the jaw, then promptly shot him. And Hubbard was right, the War Wolves took no prisoners. They killed all ten of the Khmer Rouge.

At first Lovea didn't recognize Mick (probably because of his beard; he hadn't shaved in weeks) when she came to cut him and Hubbard loose, but when he said her name she was taken aback by the sight of her old friend whom she finally recognized.

"Oh my God, Mick! How, how, how," she stammered with excitement. "How are you a prisoner of the Khmer Rouge? Why, why are you in Cambodia again? I thought you went back to Illinois."

"I took another job with Voice of America accompanying an American task force that's looking for the remains of M.I.A.s in Vietnam, Cambodia and Laos. I was separated from the group and was captured by the Khmer Rouge."

"Lucky they didn't kill you," Lovea said.

"There were times when I wish they had."

"I'm Jim Hubbard. I'm one of the missing in action the task force was looking for."

"How long have you been a prisoner?' Lovea asked.

"Mick tells me four years, if this is 1977."

"You two want to go back to Vietnam, right?"

"Yes," Mick and Hubbard said in unison.

"Okay, we'll escort you back. First we will bury our dead." "Lovea. Where is Colonel Yon?" Mick asked.

"He is dead too, killed in a firefight." She quickly changed the subject. "Are you men hungry? We have salted rat."

"You've come a long way since lizards, Lovea," Mick said, harking back to when she was hiding in the wine cellar of the Hotel Angkor in Phnom Penh.

"Oh yes. I still eat them when necessary. I see that the Khmer Rouge have a pot of rice cooked. We'll eat that with the rat before we march on to Vietnam."

After they ate, and their fellow fighters were buried, Lovea led the War Wolves and Mick and Hubbard back down the trail the Khmer Rouge had hacked through the jungle which led to a worn trail that circuvented a waterfall along a narrow river where Mick saw the boulders between which his foot had been stuck. They were on the right track toward the main Ho Chi Minh Trail, he knew -- then they wound up in a clearing where Mick's original hammock was hung. This is where he had become separated from the task force before wandering off to investigate the waterfall. Thankfully they had bypassed the place where Mick had discovered the six skeletons of the missing LURPS -- which would probably have been too traumatic for Hubbard to see.

Mick still had the teeth and corresponding dog tags in his pockets, but he had left his tape recorder behind thinking he'd return; instead he'd wound up in captivity. He'd have to report on the task force after the fact, once he got back to Voice of America in Rangoon, if he ever did.

The War Wolves were concerned about encountering Vietnamese troops in Cambodia. They could easily be mistaken for Khmer Rouge unless the Vietnamese noticed the Caucasian faces of Lovea, Mick and Hubbard first -- and apparently they did when they suddenly came face-to-face with each other on the Trail. It was a standoff at first, before each concluded that neither were Khmer Rouge. In a sense, although the Vietnamese were invading Cambodia, they and the War Wolves were allies because they were both intent on ousting Pol Pot. The Vietnamese came to understand, through a combination of broken English and French what the mission of the PRA was. Satisfied that their mission was the same, the Vietnamese moved on.

Chapter 20

Lovea and Mick walked together a short distance from the encampment and talked about what she envisioned for Cambodia's future.

"We will be free of Pol Pot and the Khmer Rouge when the Vietnamese chase them away, then they will give the PRA a voice in a new occupation government until the Cambodians govern themselves entirely after the Vietnamese leave," Lovea contended. "They will not stay in Cambodia very long. They will withdraw to protect themselves from China. I predict there will be a war between the two soon, they are so suspicious of each other. It goes back centuries since the Chinese have invaded Vietnam several times only to be thwarted in the end. And ethnic Chinese who remained behind after the invasions have long been persecuted. So there is great animosity between the two."

"But why does Vietnam want to invade Cambodia?" Mick asked.

"It's all based on mutual paranoia. You see, Pol Pot fears that a traditionally expansionist Vietnam will invade Cambodia as it did centuries before when it confiscated the Mekong River Delta," Lovea said. "Yet it was Pol Pot who initiated incursions by the Khmer Rouge into Vietnam, and he's killed thousands of Vietnamese nationals living in Cambodia. As a result, the Vietnamese, fearing an expansionist Pol Pot, have decided to respond with aggression by attacking the Khmer Rouge on Cambodian soil, which I believe is a prelude to an all out invasion by the Vietnamese to depose Pol Pot."

Hubbard, who had been walking directly behind Lovea and Mick overheard what she said, and he confirmed her contention that the Vietnamese were about to invade Cambodia.

"They are coming across the border in ever-increasing numbers. As a LURP I was assigned to observe the North Vietnamese coming into South Vietnam on the Ho Chi Minh Trail; now they're traveling on it in the opposite direction, farther and farther into Khmer Rouge territory. We're in between, and if we don't get out of here soon, I'm afraid we'll be caught in a crossfire."

"We're about a day and a half from Vietnam now," Lovea said.

Chapter 21

After another day on the Trail Hubbard's fears came to pass. The War Wolves found themselves hunkering down in the middle of a withering firefight between Vietnamese and Khmer Rouge that involved mortars being fired by both sides. A couple of them fell short among the War Wolves who scattered in all directions as shrapnel sprayed all around. Mick could hear it ripping through the trees as he and Hubbard lay flat on the ground. When there was a brief lull, they got up and ran. When Mick last saw Lovea she was scrambling for cover in the opposite direction. Hubbard and Mick continued running until they came out of the jungle into an open expanse of sun-splashed rolling hills and scrub and pine. On one of the hills was a village that resembled the Jeh's Dak Pek. They had come out in Vietnam, and soon, as they walked, out of breath from running, they encountered a Montagnard woman on a dirt road hauling firewood in a sling on her back.

"Americans," Mick said. She smiled broadly when she noticed the brass Montagnard bracelets on Mick's arms, and she motioned for them to follow her up the road to the village. She escorted them to a hut where she called out. Soon an old man appeared in the doorway. "Americans," the woman said, and the man smiled, nodded and offered his hand.

Hubbard communicated with him in pantomime and pidgin English that he and Mick had been prisoners of war in Cambodia and they wanted to get to Saigon. The old man communicated in return that they should hitchhike on nearby Highway 14 which would take them to Plieku then all the way south to Saigon. Then he placed his hand on Mick's arm and put fingers to his mouth indicating that he wanted to feed them. He motioned for the woman, who had been standing by, to bring food. She returned a short time later with bowls of rice and corn, and bananas and eggs and some kind of meat, the most food Mick had seen in weeks -- for Hubbard, years. The old man and woman watched them eat, nodding and smiling with approval, knowing they were famished the way they gobbled the food down. After they ate the woman pointed to the sores around Mick's and Hubbard's wrists, and Hubbard's ankles. She took them by hand to her hut where she soaked strips of palm leaves in rice wine and applied them to the wounds. They stuck like tape, and it stung like hell, but the alcohol would help prevent infection, Mick figured.

Mick still wore boots, but Hubbard was barefooted, and the Montagnards kindly fitted him with sandals of recycled tire treads and leather straps -- popular among GIs during the war -- and a bush jacket and pants that an American missionary had left behind after the war. Then they went their merry way down Highway 14.

Mick had hitchhiked frequently throughout the Midwest during his brief college days to party with friends who were attending various universities before he went to war, but he and another ex-GI hitchhiking in the middle of Vietnam after the war was an entirely different matter. The traffic was sparse and they walked a good ten miles before anyone stopped. It was a big Vietnamese army truck with several soldiers on board. The soldiers, chattering in Vietnamese and broken Russian, helped them up onto the truck. Apparently the soldiers thought they were Soviets. The soldiers stared at them, perhaps curious about their beards. Soviet advisers in Vietnam didn't wear beards. Then one of them pointed at Hubbard's tire tread sandals and exclaimed, "G.I.!"

"*Beaucoup* long time ago," Hubbard said. "Prisoner of war of Khmer Rouge four years, escape days ago."

The soldiers understood.

"Khmer Rouge Number 10," another of the soldiers said. "Vietnamese *cocky dow beacoup*!" meaning, Mick remembered from being in Vietnam before, that the Vietnamese considered the Khmer Rouge to be very bad and they would kill many of them.

Hubbard and Mick smiled and nodded their approval.

Here they were, two G.I.s -- albeit ex-G.I.s -- siding with the Vietnamese who were planning to invade a neighboring country, confirming the worst fears of the Domino Theory, a fear that had motivated the U.S. to go to war with the Vietnamese Communists in the first place. Approving Vietnam's invasion of Cambodia? Hardly a position that would reflect Washington's sentiments. Surely though, they wouldn't be in favor of allowing Pol Pot's bloodbath to continue.

Chapter 22

Riding along with the Vietnamese soldiers in their open-air truck in the breezy sunlight through the vast expanse of the Central Highlands felt good to Mick after spending months confined to the shady (although suffocatingly hot), damp jungle, rarely seeing the sun.

After a little more than an hour the truck stopped at a fork in the road near Ban Me Thuot where Highway 21 veered east from southbound 14 to Da Lat, as the sign said. The soldiers pointed down 14. "Saigon," they said, ignoring the fact that the city's name had been changed to Ho Chi Minh City.

Mick and Hubbard got off the truck, which headed east.

It was past noon and Mick hoped they'd reach Saigon before dark. If they got a ride soon, they'd make it with time to spare. What they'd do then -- well that was a different story. They had no money for a hotel, and Hubbard needed medical attention; he was very weak. As a last resort, or first, they could go to the Soviet Embassy and seek some assistance there. For the sake of diplomacy, perhaps the Soviets would be willing to put them up for a night or two until they could figure out what to do. Ideally they'd then fly to Manila, and go to Clark Air Force Base, where they'd be debriefed and Hubbard could be hospitalized. Mick still had the teeth and dog tags of the missing LURPS. He'd turn them over to intelligence to be officially identified.

Their next ride came in the form of an old beat-up bus that was loaded with passengers. There was room on the roof to ride with some others. Mick climbed onboard, then he helped Hubbard up.

They had no money to pay for the ride, but the driver seemed unconcerned. Maybe they'd be asked to pay when they got to Saigon, at which time Mick would offer his brass bracelets in exchange.

The bus went slowly so as not to spill any of the passengers and their belongings off the roof. The road was smooth and straight, with very little traffic, as they traveled through the sparsely-populated plains, but it grew busier as they came to one village after another, looking very much like the suburbs of a large city. They were approaching Saigon from the north where Highway 14 merged into 13. Occasionally the bus stopped to let people off and to take on new passengers. Gradually the narrow, two lane highway became a wide boulevard in the city, and after a few more blocks Mick recognized the former American Embassy, now abandoned. It was as good a place as any to hop off the bus when it slowed for traffic without the driver knowing. The Soviet Embassy would be in the vicinity. The jump down caused Hubbard to fall on his hands and knees. He was very weak, suffering from malnutrition. Mick helped him to his feet and they walked around until they found the Soviet Embassy. Knowing some Russian, Mick talked the guards into letting them in to see a consul. When he explained the circumstances which had led Hubbard and him to Saigon, the consul was very understanding, and in a surprising act of good will he gave them enough money for two nights in a hotel and a flight to Manila that was scheduled to leave in three days. The embassy nurse also examined Hubbard, and she determined that he needed to be hospitalized, but that would have to wait until they got to Clark in the Phillippines. Meanwhile, Mick put Hubbard to bed in the room they got at the stately old Continental Hotel in downtown Saigon, and he ordered soup and bananas and grapefruit for the two of them. After they ate Mick thirsted for some red wine to fortify his blood, or simply to change his state of mind which was presently rather depressed, as the psyche doesn't do well when the body is malnourished.

He left Hubbard to rest, went downstairs to the veranda and ordered a glass of wine. He had drunk on the legendary Continental's veranda ten years before when he was a G.I. watching people passing by on Tu Do Street, which intersected with a side street at the hotel. Things had changed, most notably absent were G.I.s, street walkers and the flashing neon lights of American-style bars. As in Hanoi, there was a strain on the faces of the people passing by. Post-war Nam seemed to be just as stressful in the south as in the north. Communism was failing, although the Soviets who were drinking and eating at the hotel seemed to be living a pretty good life. Normally reserved they were having a good time under the influence of vodka, so it appeared in the glasses. It certainly wasn't water making them laugh so much. One of them, a tall, lean man with short blond hair, approached Mick's table.

"I saw you in the embassy today," he said in broken English. "They say you were an American prisoner of war."

Hubbard had truly been a prisoner of war, but Mick had never thought of himself as one, but being a captive of the Khmer Rouge for a short time qualified him as such, he supposed.

"I guess you could say that," Mick said.

"A prisoner of the Vietnamese?" the Soviet asked.

"No, the Khmer Rouge."

"How were you liberated?"

"By a group of Cambodian counterinsurgency commandos called the People's Republican Army."

"Oh yes, the PRA. They are very famous for being led by a woman."

"They are famous in Vietnam?" Mick asked with surprise.

"The Vietnamese consider them an important ally in fighting against the Khmer Rouge."

"I find it to be very ironic that they are fighting each other when they were allies in the American War," Mick said.

"They are suspicious of each other's ambitions. Much like your country and mine. We were allies once, in World War II. Now we are very suspicious of each other's ambitions. That's what the Cold War is all about. Each side accuses the other of being the aggressor, based on the number of nuclear warheads in their respective arsenals," the Soviet said smiling.

"This is why the SALT Treaties are so important, to strike a balance of power so that neither side has the advantage. Then all that remains will serve as a mutual deterrent to keep us from blowing the Earth off its axis in a nuclear war. In the spirit of detente I would like to buy you another wine."

"Certainly," Mick said.

Then Mick bought the Soviet a drink and the conversation shifted from the arms race to lighter subjects like the gold medal race at the Olympic Games of 1976 and the space race. And Mick graciously conceded that the Soviets were the first to leave the Earth's atmosphere in a Sputnik, and he said that he hoped someday the U.S. and the U.S.S.R. would man an international space station instead of developing space weaponry to be deployed against each other in a kind of star war.

After a couple more drinks apiece, Mick and the Soviet parted company, and Mick went back upstairs to the room to check on Hubbard. He had fallen fast asleep. Mick took one of the pillows and slept on the floor. In the morning Mick awoke with Hubbard standing over him.

"I feel better, how about you?" he asked with a snicker knowing that Mick had gone downstairs to drink and he probably had a hangover.

"Not bad, considering. I sure could use some food, though. Anything left?"

"Yeah, if you can stomach cold egg drop soup."

The thought of it made Mick feel sicker.

"No thanks. Let's go find something else for breakfast."

They went out and found a street vendor who was selling pocket sandwiches – French bread stuffed with some kind of meat. Mick hoped it wasn't dog. As desperate as the Vietnamese were for food these days, it very well could have been. But then again, they had always eaten dog.

Chapter 23

Mick and Hubbard had another day and night to kill before catching the flight to Manila. Mick was inclined to kill the time drinking on the veranda with the Soviets. Detente was addictive. He spoke their language to a certain extent, and he was interested in gaining insight into their culture and the way they viewed Americans. He invited Hubbard to join them but Hubbard declined, not wanting to hobnob with Communists; he had been in their company long enough. When Mick arrived on the veranda the Soviets were leaving. They bid each other good evening and Mick sat at a table and ordered a bottle of "33"; Vietnam's most popular beer during the war, and apparently it still was. He noticed three or four bottles of it being drunk by Vietnamese men at a couple of the tables.

The veranda wasn't very crowded as it had been during the war years when foreigners of all kinds came there to consort.

Mick's waiter looked bored standing off to the side, waiting for someone to order a drink, but Mick kept him busy enough until almost closing time when everyone else had left. Feeling friendly, Mick engaged him in conversation the next time he brought him a beer.

"What's your name?" he asked the waiter, who responded a little shyly.

"Trung Phu. Your name, please"

"Mick Scott."

"You are American?"

"Yes."

"Why you in Vietnam now?"

Mick explained.

"Hope all missing Americans go home someday," Trung said sympathetically. "Vietnamese too. Many are still away."

"You are South Vietnamese or North Vietnamese?" Mick asked.

"First North. I come here in 1954 from Hanoi..." He looked around over his shoulder and spoke in a low tone, "...when Communist take over there. Afraid to lose freedom like people in South have now. Now Vietnam same same North and South."

He looked over his shoulder again and spoke even lower, bending closer to Mick.

"Times are very hard in Vietnam now. My wife who is tailor, you know, sew, sew, can't make living now. You know *ao dai*?"

"*Ao dai*? The dress? Ah, yes."

Mick remembered them well. His Vietnamese girlfriend, Tron, had worn them; the high-collared, colorful dress that was split up the sides almost to the waist, with silk pantaloons, usually white or black, worn underneath. With her long, black, silky hair, she looked beautiful in lavender *ao dais* and white pantaloons, like a swallow-tailed butterfly.

"They are outlawed now," Trung said.

"No."

"Yes. Considered too bourgeois by Communist. *Ao dai* was the bulk of her business, very, what you say, lucrative, but private profit they see as anti-revolutionary. Now wife cleans barracks of soldiers, wash their clothes for *ti ti* piaster. Along with what I earn here, just enough for some rice every day, maybe duck or chicken, two a month. Barely keep roof overhead. Vietnamese very poor now. Many thousand leave on secret boats for Hong Kong, Australia, Phillippines. Some drown, eat by sharks, attack by pirates."

"Will you leave on a boat, Trung?"

"If I save enough piaster to get to Da Nang where boats leave."

"Maybe this will help."

Not having extra money, Mick gave Trung one of his Montagnard bracelets.

"Brass will fetch a few dollars on the black market, I'm sure," Mick said.

Trung smiled broadly, bowed to Mick and they shook hands goodbye.

Chapter 24

In the morning, after eating the last grapefruits, Mick and Hubbard took a cyclo -- a two-person buggy attached to the front of a bicycle -- to Tan Son Nhut Airport on the northern edge of Saigon. Mick had taken this route many times after a night on Tu Do Street during the war. He had lived in a villa not far from the front gate of Tan Son Nhut, just off Tru Minh Ky Street. It was in this neighborhood that he had met Tron at her father's corner bakery near the villa. They had a typical boyfriend/girlfriend relationship; going to the zoo on Sundays, dinner out, movies, not the bawdy bar girl/drunken GI relationship that was all too typical during the war.

Thinking of his relationship with Tron made him think of Kathy back home. He had left her in the lurch caring for his pets. He had been gone much longer than planned. It seemed like ten years. Would she understand?

Hubbard had been gone much longer than planned. Mick asked him how it felt to be going home.

"I'm concerned that my wife won't know me anymore, and my son doesn't know his father. He was only six months old when I left. He's what, about five now? She probably gave up on me being found alive. What if she's remarried? What then?"

"That would be a difficult situation to be in, I must admit," Mick said.

"I should have been killed along with the others. Why in the hell did I survive anyway, and they didn't. What's so special about me?"

"Don't question fate, Jim. It was meant to be that way. Now your son will know his father."

"Yes, yes he will, thanks to the Good Lord."

"Sounds like you're a man of God, Jim."

"My belief in God is what sustained me through my ordeal. I prayed to him often, and in return he gave me the faith that someday I'd go free. My prayers were answered. Are you a believer, Mick?"

"My belief was shaken when I witnessed the bloodbath in Cambodia. I wondered how a benevolent God could create a monster like Pol Pot, and I came to the conclusion that man himself is responsible for such evil behavior. Because of the human brain, which was designed by God, I believe, we are capable of choosing between good and evil. But when circumstances arise that man has no control over, then God has the power to intervene.

"When I was trapped between those two boulders in the jungle before I stumbled upon you, I prayed too, calling on God to release me, and he did. And when we were held captive I prayed again, and again divine intervention came into play in the form of Lovea Duval and the War Wolves."

"Yeah," Hubbard said, "she's an angel, I believe."

Chapter 25

It was the second time Mick had lifted off from Vietnam, and it was the third time he had flown to the Phillippines. The first time was during the war when he went there for escape and evasion and jungle survival school. He had survived and escaped the jungle all right, but nearly ten years after he had left the war, Vietnam's with the U.S. Now they were having another with Cambodia, and would soon be at war with their long-time nemesis China, Cambodia's staunch ally. Mick read about it in the *Pacific Stars & Stripes* newspaper when he arrived at Clark Air Force Base. The article said that Vietnam's relations with China had deteriorated to the point where the two had been on the verge of war for months. The dispute, the article said, was a direct result of the long quarrel between China (an ally of Cambodia) and the Soviet Union (an ally of Vietnam) and Peking's suspicions that Hanoi was cooperating with Moscow's efforts to encircle China with a cordon of hostile states. Vietnam's nationalization of small businesses in the South, particularly in Saigon -- enterprises that have traditionally been the domain of ethnic Chinese living in Vietnam -- coupled with reports of officially sanctioned harassment of the Chinese, had further exacerbated the situation. China claimed that the nationalization action was designed to punish persons of Chinese ancestry for Peking's backing of Pol Pot. The Peking-Hanoi dispute was also aggrivated by the Vietnam-Cambodian conflict which found several thousand Vietnamese troops occupying several miles of Cambodian territory. This followed more than two years of skirmishing, which most neutral observers thought was initiated by the Khmer Rouge, as they suspected Vietnam of planning to reduce Cambodia to a tributary state, based on Hanoi's stated intention to supplant France as the dominate power in Indochina. Conversely, Vietnam suspected that Cambodia's ultimate goal was to regain all of the fertile Mekong Delta from the Vietnamese who had confiscated it years before. As a result, a paranoid Hanoi launched a full-scale invasion of Cambodia while counterinsurgents like Lovea Duval's People's Republican Army attacked Pol Pot's forces from within. Together, along with other rebel forces, in December of 1978, the Vietnamese captured Phnom Penh and sent Pol Pot scurrying into the countryside with remnants of the Khmer Rouge. In August of 1979 Pol Pot was convicted and sentenced to death in absentia by a court in Phnom Penh for the death of thousands of former officials and soldiers of the Lon Nol administration which had been overthrown by the Khmer Rouge four years before, the article pointed out.

Yet, shockingly, in September of 1979, the UN General Assembly voted overwhelmingly to continue to recognize Pol Pot's right to Cambodia's UN seat.

The Vietnamese would pay a price for the invasion of Cambodia. In retaliation, in February of 1979, China, Pol Pot's staunchest ally, attacked Vietnam along its northern border with an estimated 250,000 troops who were met with fierce resistance containing the invasion to within 20 to 25 miles inside the country. The month-long war cost both sides many causalities. Peking reported 20,000 Chinese were killed and wounded; Vietnam's casualties numbered some 50,000.

Chapter 26

After leaving Vietnam, Mick was united in the Phillippines with Waterman and the rest of the task force -- along with Jake Damphier who had financed the missions. They had remained at Clark awaiting the results of forensic examinations of the remains of the missing Americans they had recovered in Cambodia, Laos and Vietnam.

"When you became separated from us we looked for you for three days," Waterman said. "We imagined the worst when we couldn't find you, remembering what Xuan, our guide, said about North Vietnamese Army troops who had been separated from their units on the Ho Chi Minh Trail being killed by tigers. That, or we thought you might have been swept away in that raging river near the encampment."

Mick explained what had happened – that he'd been trapped by the boulders at the foot of the waterfall.

"I screamed for help but you apparently couldn't hear me because of the roar of the water."

"We weren't aware of any waterfall, only the river. "I'm sorry, Mick."

"All's well that ends well," Mick said. "I discovered the remains of the missing LURPS and their lone survivor, Major Jim Hubbard. He's in the base hospital now. We were held captive by the Khmer Rouge before being liberated by the Cambodian People's Republican Army. Heard of 'em?"

"No, but there are a few anti-Pol Pot insurgents operating in Cambodia I'm told," Waterman said.

"Here are the remains, just teeth and the corresponding dog tags."

"Amazing. We searched all over Hill 61 for some sign of the LURPS. Where were they?" Waterman inquired.

"Below the eastern slope of a hill down in a valley. Could have been Hill 61, I don't know."

Damphier read the dog tags. "That's them all right, but we'll need to talk to Hubbard for further confirmation. Great work, Mick, you deserve a medal for this. I'll get you a voucher for clothes and toiletries at the base exchange, feed you in a chow hall and put you up in a barracks tonight so you can shower; then we'll get you on a plane for home ASAP. The ticket's on us. Where do you want to fly?"

"St. Louis would be the closest major airport to my home in Carbondale, Illinois; I was going to fly to Rangoon first, to give Voice of America a report on the task force, but I lost my tape recorder and tapes in the jungle. Do you think you could arrange for me to use the facilities of Clark's Armed Forces Radio station to do a report? I could feed it to Voice of America from here, via satellite."

"I'll see what I can do. By the way, how are you fixed for cash."

"I don't have any."

"Here's fifty bucks; you'll need it to rent a car or to take a bus from St. Louis to Carbondale."

Damphier arranged for Mick to use the Armed Forces Radio facilities at Clark, where Mick recorded a report on the task force for Voice of America. In a nutshell it described how congenial the Vietnamese were in allowing the Americans to search for the remains of their soldiers missing in action from the war, when they themselves were still missing thousands. And he touched upon the difficulties the task force faced traversing mountainous jungle to reach the isolated sites where U.S. soldiers and airmen had gone missing, and the tedious and laborious task of finding and recovering those remains after several years of exposure to the elements. Without minimizing his role in finding the remains of the missing LURPS, he simply said they were found by a member of the task force, and in the process, one of the LURPs, U.S. Marine Major Jim Hubbard, who had been captured by the Khmer Rouge, was freed by Cambodian counterinsurgents after four long years of captivity. The happy ending to his story.

PART 2

Chapter 27

The happy ending to Mick's story was that he was finally flying home. His return flight to the U.S. included stops in Honolulu, Los Angeles and St. Louis, where he rented a car to drive to Carbondale. Mick enjoyed the drive through southern Illinois, not being in hostile territory anymore. He was down home in the good ole peaceful U.S. of A., although, being in the middle of summer, it was just as hot as Cambodia and Vietnam. He could hardly wait to get to his cool, stone house on Lake Wells where a breeze always blew over the water. He would be glad to see Kathy too, and his dog and cat. He had missed them, and although he had found female companionship in Lovea, it had been strictly platonic. He longed for Kathy's sensuous touch, the feel of her lips on his. He longed for her smell – the natural perfume of her femininity that he savored when they embraced, and the sight of her big blue eyes that gleamed like sapphires when she smiled.

Carmella, his golden retriever, must have sensed Mick was coming. She met him on the path that wound through the woods toward the house, tail wagging furiously, whimpering, wanting to be petted. When they got to the house Mick opened the door hoping to see Kathy there, but no one was home, except Jazzpur the cat who rubbed up against Mick's leg and meowed.

Kathy must have been in Carbondale. She worked there as a counselor at the Phoenix House, a drug and alcohol rehabilitation facility.

Mick climbed up to the loft. The bed was neatly made. A summery dress was draped on a chair, and on the night stand was a clear glass vase containing wild flowers.

The bed looked inviting. Mick was suffering from a severe case of jet lag. He lay down and immediately drifted off to sleep, until he heard someone coming up the ladder to the loft. Kathy appeared. She smiled.

"Hi, Mick. Welcome home."

She sat on the bed and held his hand. He pulled her down and kissed her. She lay down beside him.

"I read in *Time Magazine* about what's been happening over there. You must have been in grave danger," she said.

"All foreigners were, but because they thought I was with Radio Moscow reporting on their agricultural revolution, they cut me some slack, until one of my tapes destined for Voice of America was intercepted. Then they tried to kill me and the others who were involved in smuggling the tapes out of the country. The tapes revealed Khmer Rouge atrocities."

"Tried to kill you? How?"

"Shot us down in a plane when we tried to fly to Rangoon. We survived a crash landing in western Cambodia and were rescued by a U.S. Air Force chopper flying out of a base in Thailand."

"Sounds harrowing, was anybody hurt?"

"Pich Sabay, my Cambodian friend, was killed."

"Sorry."

Kathy rested her head on Mick's chest. "I really missed you," she whispered.

"I missed you." And they kissed passionately and Mick rolled over on top of her and they made up for lost time.

Chapter 28

Lost time for sure. The last two years seemed as if he'd spent it in the Twilight Zone from the moment he set foot in Rangoon, to the moment he touched down in St. Louis the day before. The title of the book he wrote about Vietnam, *Like Another Lifetime in Another World* seemed apropos to what he had just gone through. He wanted to forget about it all, so he drank to drown the memories, but they always came back to him in his dreams. He dreamt of the skulls of Kampong Cham and the skeletons of the LURPS, and of being trapped between the boulders again, and his harrowing captivity at the hands of the Khmer Rouge.

And it became a problem with Kathy, a recovering alcoholic. She didn't like sleeping with a drunk who woke up in the middle of the night in a cold sweat from bad dreams, so she moved back to Carbondale.

It was the second time in their relationship that she had moved out because of his drinking. After the first time he had been sober for a year before he went to Washington to prepare for his assignment to Cambodia. Kathy didn't know that he had fallen off the wagon there. And that he had drunk wine with Lovea in Phnom Penh, rice wine with the Montagnards in Nam, and vodka with the Soviets in Saigon. It hadn't been a problem though, until he came home, but the problem wasn't really the alcohol perse', but the rather post traumatic stress that had followed him home, causing him to use alcohol to treat this newly-diagnosed disorder, a reaction to war-time experiences. Veterans of wars before Vietnam didn't have the luxury of this diagnosis; they were left to readjust to peacetime society without the benefit of legitimate medical reasons as to why they couldn't. They were simply considered nut cases or alcoholics.

Mick began hanging out at The Club again, a bar on Illinois Avenue in Carbondale, where Vietnam vets drank. It was owned by his old buddy John, a former Sea Bee who had helped him build his stone house. On occasional Saturday nights, because the bar was closed on Sundays, they'd get a bottle of whiskey at closing time and go out to Mick's and drink. Hangover notwithstanding, this proved to be mutually therapeutic as they talked about their war experiences. Mick sorely missed Kathy, though – there was nothing more therapeutic than a healthy roll in the sack. How beautiful she looked lying on the bed in the loft with the soft golden light shining through the yellow glass skylight on her bare breasts, a vision that sustained him on the long, lonely nights when he went to bed alone, and sometimes sober. Yes, he was sober sometimes, and when he was he accomplished a lot, writing his second book. It was the story of Lovea, but he didn't yet know how it would end. He didn't know what had happened to her since he last saw her in the jungle, scrambling for her life.

If she had survived, with the Vietnamese invading Cambodia, her fate could very well rest with them -- if they successfully overthrew Pol Pot and the Khmer Rouge. Would she and the People's Republican Army be included in a new occupation government, since they had fought against the Khmer Rouge too? Or perhaps she had sought refuge in Vietnam as many Cambodians and Mick and Hubbard had. Whatever her fate, Mick hoped that someday he'd know what it was, for the sake of a happy ending for his book. He hoped it would be a story of survival.

Chapter 29

Mick spent the rest of summer trying to regain some of the weight he had lost while virtually starving in Cambodia. He had never appreciated food so much -- food and freedom, two precious commodities that most Americans took for granted. He had learned that they were scarce in countries with Communist governments. Why so much of the third world had adopted this form of government was beyond Mick's comprehension. Revolutionaries like Castro, Lenin, Stalin, Ho Chi Minh, Pol Pot and Mao had a romantic, but foolhardy notion that it would lead to a utopia through collectivism, but in reality it only led to collective misery, and in most cases, mass murder. The numbers of those murdered in Cambodia under Pol Pot, for example, had now reached millions, as it had under Stalin in the USSR, and in Red China with Mao. Admittedly, in Vietnam there had not been the anticipated bloodbath when the Communists took over -- except during the infamous Tet Offensive of 1968 when they slaughtered thousands of civilians at Hue for not siding with them against the Allies.

At any rate, Mick was damned glad to be back home in America, fat, sassy, relatively happy and free. He was free all right. He didn't have to work, having been paid handsomely for his work with the CIA -- and royalties from his first book trickled in periodically. He had plenty of spare time to work on his second book, and with fall and winter coming, he spent time chopping wood for the fireplace, his only source of heat. And he enjoyed sitting in the sauna he and John had built. John sometimes came out to use it too, on Sundays, with his girlfriend, but Mick grew tired of being the odd man out, so he concentrated on finding a girlfriend for himself, which would entail going to other bars besides The Club, where very few women drank.

He went to Merlin's across the street, a live music joint that catered to students as well as townies. Mick had become a townie himself, after graduate school. It was there that he met another townie one night – a hot, buxom redhead named Alice. They danced, and Mick bought her a drink, and they tried to talk over the music, but it was too loud, so they went up the street to a quieter place called P.K.'s, an acronym for Pizza King, which had long ceased selling pizzas. Now it was basically a pool hall that served booze. They got two beers at the bar then sat in a booth in a remote, dark corner.

The clientele at P.K.'s consisted primarily of those who appeared to be clinging to the '60s – aging hippies, a population for which Carbondale was known, former students (grads and dropouts) who had stayed in the area which was considered a liberal oasis an otherwise conservative southern Illinois.   Carbondale had been a hotbed for the anti-Vietnam War movement whose many demonstrators had turned violent in the name of peace. This was the subject of the conversation between Mick and Alice, the hypocrisy of the liberal movement – or at least that's what it seemed like from Mick's perspective. Alice saw it differently.

"Sometimes civil disobedience is necessary."

"Like not wearing a bra," Mick said, attempting to lighten the conversation.

Alice laughed. "I suppose that's a form of it."

"And a very nice form it is," Mick observed indiscreetly, while looking at her breasts.

"You're bold," Alice said. "I like that in a man. Do you like bold women?"

She pushed her hand up Mick's thigh, looked in his eyes and smiled, and they kissed, then she took his hand and put it on one of her breasts beneath her sweater, and she said, "I like it on top."

"Let's go out to my house before we get too drunk," Mick suggested.

"Out? Where do you live?" Alice inquired.

"Lake Wells."

"My house is closer. I live on West Cherry, 445."

"Okay, I'll meet you there," Mick said, anxious to see just how bold this woman could be.

It didn't take him long to find out. As soon as they got inside she threw her arms around him, pressing her body tight against his, then they fell together onto the couch, she on top of him. Straddling his hips she gracefully discarded her sweater and skirt; she wasn't wearing panties. She then unzipped his pants and pulled them down to his ankles. Mounting him she achieved penetration while dangling her breasts in his face. He kissed them while caressing her buttocks as she moved up and down, moaning with pleasure.

Mick tried his best to keep up, thrusting his pelvis up to meet her, then she began to quiver and pant until she became breathless; gasping for air, she threw her head back and screeched, then she collapsed, sweating on his chest. It was the most intense orgasmic display Mick had ever witnessed, unless she was faking it; if so, she deserved an Oscar.

Mick managed to slip out from beneath her while she drifted off to sleep, a little drunk and exhausted from the sex.

Although Mick had not had an orgasm himself, he was content that he had satisfied the woman first, an achievement not easily attained by men who suffered from premature ejaculation. It was an affliction women complained about endlessly, primarily in *Cosmopolitan Magazine*.

In this particular case it was the woman who had the hair trigger.

Chapter 30

One night stands notwithstanding, Mick was dissatisfied with his relationships with women. He he'd had good ones with Lovea, although platonic, and with Kathy, with whom he'd been very intimate. He missed and thought about both of them often. Lovea's whereabouts remained a mystery, whereas he knew where to find Kathy -- at the Phoenix House in Carbondale. He considered going there to talk things out with her, but he'd have to give up alcohol first, and he wasn't ready to. He enjoyed drinking too much with John and the boys at The Club.

Once in awhile a couple of them came out to the lake with John on Sundays to fish for bass. Lake Wells was known for containing big ones. Mick had caught one to prove it – an eight pound beauty that he had mounted above the fireplace. John was jealous of it, and vowed to catch a bigger one, so they decided to have a contest. The loser would buy a keg for a party in the fall. John was so determined to win that he bought a small john boat with a trolling motor so he could fish from deeper water. Not to be outdone, Mick occasionally rented one from the marina across the lake from his house.

Floating around on the lake, Mick reflected on an episode that had occurred there four years before, after he had been discovered infiltrating the Students for a Democratic Society (SDS) and its militant faction, the Weather Underground. It was his first CIA assignment.

The Vietnamese Studies Center on the campus of Southern Illinois University in Carbondale had become the focus of the Weather Underground's anger because it was thought to be affiliated with the CIA, which it was; David Gordon, the Center's director, was an agent who recruited Mick to infiltrate the Underground.

It later came to light that the Center itself had been infiltrated by none other than Gordon's wife, who turned out to be a North Vietnamese spy. He'd met her at the CIA office in Saigon during the early years of the war when he was in charge thr. She had posed as a secretary. Upon being outed at the Cente she fled Carbondale back to Saigon, then up the Ho Chi Minh Trail to Hanoi, her original home. Before she left Carbondale, however, she exposed Mick by pilfering Center files that contained information about his role in infiltrating the Weather Underground. She turned the files over to their leader, Stuart Bolshinsky, and subsequently some attempts were made on Mick's life.

The leader of Carbondale's Black Panthers, Marcus Jackson, who was an ally of the Weather Underground, sought revenge on Mick for exposing their plan to bomb the Center, so he stalked Mick and was suspected of blowing up his house in Carbondale before he built the one at Lake Wells.

At Lake Wells Jackson stalked Mick from a boat, watching his every move from afar through binoculars. Jackson, Mick thought, was planning to bomb his lake home too, approaching it from the water so he wouldn't have to risk carrying a volatile bomb through rugged woods at night.

Instead of notifying the police, who were familiar with Jackson, Mick took matters into his own hands. He got a hold of a Navy Seal handbook on scuba diving and underwater demolition. He ordered the necessary diving equipment through an Army/Navy Surplus catalogue, and he purchased explosives from a nearby construction company, then he lay in wait every night along the shore in a position from where he could intercept Jackson if he approached the house in a straight line from the marina.

On the third night Jackson sped across the water in the anticipated path from the marina toward Mick's house. Mick swam out to meet him. He timed it perfectly, slapped a bomb on the bottom of Jackson's boat, and ten seconds later, as Mick swam away, the bomb went off. A secondary explosion indicated that another bomb had been on board, killing Jackson and sinking the boat. A few days later, because Jackson hadn't returned to the marina where his car was parked, he was reported missing and presumed drowned. Mick was haunted by the fear that a body, or parts thereof, would turn up someday -- and one day they did, in the form of an arm that Carmella, the golden retriever, brought ashore. Mick had always been concerned that more body parts would surface. And they did.

Mick's bass fishing contest with John continued throughout southern Illinois' long, hot, tropical-like summer. While "going for the big one," they caught plenty of panfish that they fried ate on Sundays with cold beer. To cool off, they swam in the lake; that's where John made a morbid discovery. Hung up in a brush pile near shore, just below the surface of the water, was a human skull. John wanted to notify the police right away. Certain that the skull was Marcus Jackson's, Mick stalled. It was missing a jaw bone, a telltale sign of extreme trauma indicating the victim he had likely met with foul play. The body sure as hell wasn't in one piece, which would have been the case if he had simply drowned. If the police were called, they'd start asking questions, for example, whether Mick had known Marcus Jackson. With a little investigating they'd know that he had. They knew that Mick had infiltrated the SDS/Weather Underground, which had put him in contact with the local Black Panthers, and Jackson had been a suspect in bombing Mick's Carbondale house, so there was a definite connection through which the two could be linked.

Mick told John he'd call the police first thing in the morning, but of course he didn't dare. Meanwhile, John told the story of the skull to a patron at The Club -- who happened to be a cop who followed up on it, and he paid Mick a visit. The cop made an initial assumption that the skull could be that of Marcus Jackson, whose drowning had remained a mystery because no body had turned up when the lake was dragged. Mick knew why -- Jackson had been blown to bits, as the severed skull missing a jaw bone might indicate.

"We'll do a forensic exam," the cop said. "Based on the condition of the skull, and Jackson's history for violence -- he shot it out with us once -- it wouldn't surprise me at all if this proved to be his.

"You knew Jackson too, right?" the cop inquired knowing full well that Mick did.

"Yes," Mick admitted, but there was no way they could make a connection between him and Jackson's demise unless they got a search warrant and discovered the leftover ingredients from the bomb, and the scuba diving equipment he had stashed in the shed. He disposed of it all right away, in the lake. Now there was no evidence left linking Mick to the crime. He had gotten by with murder -- but there was guilt in his heart and it messed with his brain. He couldn't stop thinking about what he had done, though he managed to rationalize that Jackson deserved what he got because he had been intent on killing Mick. Nonetheless, the deed haunted him day and night, especially at night when he tried to sleep. And when he finally did sleep, he dreamt again of Jackson being blown to bits, and his body parts washing ashore one by one until a complete cadaver lay at his feet as the police stood by and watched -- then they arrested him for murder. Would this nightmare come to pass? Were the police really him?

Chapter 31

In June Mick got a surprise visit from David Gordon.

"We haven't forgotten about you, Mick, and all that you did in Cambodia for Voice of America, and we are aware that you discovered the remains of those missing LURPS and helped to free their lone survivor from Khmer Rouge captivity."

"It wasn't I who freed him, it was the People's Republican Army led by Lovea Duval. Are you familiar with them?" Mick asked.

"The PRA? Very much so. One of our agents helped to organize them in Thailand," David said.

"Yeah, it just so happens that I was there for its inauguration when a Colonel Yon and Lovea got together with Agent Don Young in Bangkok to work out the details," Mick informed David.

"Yon was eventually killed. Do you know what's happened to Duval? Mick asked

"She has established herself and the PRA as a legitimate voice in a coalition government that's being proposed. I predict she'll be president someday when the Vietnamese leave. She's very popular among her countrymen, having exacted revenge on the Khmer Rouge," David said, indicating that he had been keeping abreast with the current situation in Cambodia.

"It's thought that the PRA was directly responsible for sending Pol Pot into exile. They literally chased him into Thailand. He escaped by the skin of his bloodthirsty teeth. He's thought to be in China now. It's rumored that a couple of his men who were captured by the PRA said that while he was being chased out of Cambodia, he whimpered like a scared rabbit as he ran. True or false, he probably escaped in a truck or a Jeep, but it's the impression the people of Cambodia prefer to be left with."

"It's an image I enjoy visualizing," Mick said with a grin.

"Visualize this, Mick. You're at the White House receiving the Presidential Medal of Freedom."

"Now why would I want to do that?"

"Because you're being considered for the medal," David said.

"Get real, come on, you're pulling my leg."

"No, it's true. The work you did for Voice of America in reporting the atrocities in Cambodia caught the attention of the State Department. They've nominated you for the award. We'll find out in November if you've been selected."

"If I recall, David, you like whiskey. This calls for a drink. How about a shot of Jack Daniels on the rocks."

"Doesn't get much better than that, unless it's two shots."

"Comin' right up."

Well into the night David and Mick reminisced about the ant-war movement days in Carbondale in the late '60s and early '70s.

"Exciting times, Mick, but dangerous, with the Weather Underground after your ass. You taught them a thing or two though, when you bombed that Black Panther's boat."

"I'm still paranoid about being found out, David."

"I wouldn't sweat it, Mick, by now he'd be nothing but bone, and without flesh, which is rubbery and buoyant, a skeleton would sink to the bottom, where Davey Jones's locker lies," David said, making light of the situation, but Mick told him about the skull surfacing, and the arm that Carmella brought out of the lake. "If enough body parts turn up it might be determined that he died traumatically."

"If any more surface I certainly wouldn't tell the police," David said.

"They already know about the skull."

"What'd they say about that?"

"They said it could be Jackson's, but they were puzzled as to why the head was severed and it was missing a jaw bone, if he had simply drowned."

"Do they have any forensic evidence that foul play was involved?" David asked.

"Not that I know of."

"Then rest easy, my friend. Well, guess I better head into town to the motel. Gotta a pillow mint waiting for me," David said, somewhat dismissive of the situation, which pissed Mick off in a way, after all, it had been David's idea to bomb Jackson's boat.

Chapter 32

Lovea Duval was heralded as a heroine among the Cambodian people for helping the Vietnamese send Pol Pot into exile. She and the People's Republican Army, better known as the War Wolves, continued to attack diehard pockets of Khmer Rouge who remained behind in a last-ditch effort to keep their bloody agrarian revolution alive in the face of the occupying forces of Vietnam. When the last Khmer Rouge were vanquished from Phnom Penh and relegated to the countryside again, Lovea settled back in at the Hotel Angkor.

The hotel was returned to her ownership, as the beneficiary of her mother's estate, which had been dissolved under Pol Pot, but reinstated by the Vietnamese who considered her to be an ally, because she too had fought the Khmer Rouge.

The hotel's restaurant and bar became popular places for the upper echelon of the occupying Vietnamese forces to socialize, dine, and drink fine wine with the legendary War Wolf Lovea Duval. Because of her popularity and reputation as a fierce opponent of the Khmer Rouge, the Vietnamese accorded her a voice in the occupying government as a representative of the People's Republican Army -- which was transformed into the People's Republican Party. Even though she cooperated with the Vietnamese she consistently advocated, before the weekly occupying governmental assemblies, for Cambodian autonomy in an independent coalition government.

Like a lawyer arguing a case before a judge and jury in court, she was assertive, but respectful and very persuasive in contending that since Pol Pot had been deposed, the time had come for the Vietnamese to withdraw. She assured those assembled that an independent Cambodia was no threat to Vietnam. In fact, she argued that they could be valuable allies in rejuvenating the economy of Southeast Asia as a whole, restoring its previous position as one of the world's leading exporters of rice and rubber. Allies, she was quick to emphasize, with each nation respecting the other's territorial integrity and political independence.

Hanoi was listening through their man in Phnom Penh, General Vo Vu Ky, commander of occupation forces. He was sympathetic to Lovea's assertions, while the Vietnamese contemplated withdrawing from Cambodia so they could bolster their defensive forces, now stretched thinly along their northern border with China, after its invasion of Vietnam in 1979.

General Ky was more than sympathetic to Lovea; he was infatuated with her, the legendary leader of the War Wolves, and a general in her own right.

The General was a shiny-faced, portly man who was fond of consuming wine night after night at the hotel after dining on Mekong River catfish, fresh vegetables -- which had been scarce under Pol Pot. With the Vietnamese, however, came the freedom to fish again, and to grow vegetables in individual plots -- which Lovea did in the courtyard of the hotel. The vintage French wine came from the cellar of course, which had miraculously remained undiscovered throughout the Pol Pot years.

She had hidden in the wine cellar when the Khmer Rouge stormed through the capital, killing and imprisoning entrepreneurs. But Lovea had been more than an entrepreneur; she had been a columnist who was critical of the Khmer Rouge -- even before they conquered Phnom Penh. The murderous Khmer Rouge, who killed her mother while trying to find her -- even as she hid in the cellar. Her murdered mother's blood stains from the murder remained on the kitchen floor, a constant reminder of one of the reasons Lovea became a counterinsurgent. Now she was an ally of General Vu Vo Ky of the Communist Vietnamese. Strange bedfellows they did make.

Out of this alliance came a mutual desire to establish a government that would respect the autonomy of both Cambodia and Vietnam, allaying Vietnamese fears that the the Cambodians had designs on their territory, especially the rice-rich Mekong Delta that once belonged to them. This fear had driven the Vietnamese invasion and occupation of Cambodia, as the Khmer Rouge under Pol Pot had made aggressive incursions into Vietnam along the border where the Mekong fanned out into the delta, and farther north on the eastern frontier that bordered Vietnam's Central Highlands.

Lovea assured General Ky and the occupying government's assemblies that the new Cambodian government would only be interested in maintaining its present borders with Vietnam, Laos and Thailand.

Chapter 33

Lovea wrote Mick a lengthy letter inviting him to return to Cambodia to see first hand how much it was changing.

Dear Mick,

While the Vietnamese have left behind a contingent to contend with pockets of Khmer Rouge resistance, they don't interfere with the Cambodian people's domestic affairs, particularly in the realm of economics, which is primarily black market-based at the present time. In Phnom Penh, thousands scramble aboard the trains to Battambang -- enterprising traders off to buy goods, smuggled in from Thailand, to bring back for sale in the capital: soap, cigarettes, medicines and watches. In the market town of Sisophon -- not far from the Thai town of Aranyaprathet where the War Wolves were born, and a hotbed of the recovering economy -- a village entrepreneur can sell a fat pig for enough money to stock up on sandals, flashlights and batteries and cooking pots, all simple but scarce commodities since the Pol Pot days when such things were confiscated and people were forced to eat what food was available in communal kitchens. Enough inventory to keep a little crossroads stall in business for months. For big items like stereos and motorcycles, payment is commonly in gold. Surprisingly Cambodia has a quantity of gold left over from the Lon Nol days, when the U.S. flooded Cambodia with financial aid. This produced inordinate new wealth, which when added to old wealth, accumulated in the hands of corrupt officials who converted the dollars into gold and hid it away in Phnom Penh. It has surfaced in vast quantities, about a hundred million dollars worth each year since the Khmer Rouge have been gone. It's helping to drive the economy down the road to recovery, along with the reintroduction of a currency after the five years' hiatus under Pol Pot.

The Cambodian people are very enterprising, I'm proud to say, and soon we will be producing much rice and rubber for exporting, although presently little is being grown, because --sadly -- there are not enough men left alive to do the plowing. Nor are there enough oxen and buffalo. And although this year's growing season was relatively good, next year's is expected to be bad because of Mekong River flooding in some areas and drought in others.

Thankfully, UNICEF brought in a thousand Japanese, East German and British trucks, and river barges to distribute tens of thousands of tons of rice provided by the U.N.'s World Food Program (which was paid for by the United States) to feed the people.

Admittedly, the fanatical vision of Pol Pot for an agrarian utopia was based on the growing of great quantities of rice, but in his distorted view cities were useless, so he emptied them. Trade was evil, so abolish all markets -- abolish money. Abolish schools, except those that are used to brainwash the people, young and old, into thinking like Communists. Destroy contaminating Western influences like televisions and air conditioners. Destroy contaminated people -- former soldiers, teachers, physicians and entrepreneurs.

This is Pol Pot's legacy, yet remarkably, the United States and the United Nations still recognize him as a legitimate spokesman for the people of Cambodia. A travesty that has not gone unnoticed by the UN Commission on Human Rights. They've invited me to testify before them and the International Court of Justice in hopes of getting the murderous monster tried for war crimes. Perhaps, Mick, you could testify on our behalf since you witnessed some of the atrocities? Can you meet me in New York the 12th of December at the Sheraton Manhattan Hotel?

Sincerely,
Lovea

Mick wrote Lovea back saying he wouldn't be returning to Cambodia anytime soon, but that he would be happy to testify at the UN in December against Pol Pot, even though he was tired of traveling. He had wanted to settle down for awhile at Lake Wells and concentrate on writing the book about Cambodia and Lovea, but the final chapter couldn't be written until the man was brought to justice.

Chapter 34

One crisp, autumn night when Mick went outside to look at the stars -- they shone bright at Lake Wells -- he thought he saw a shadow coming through the woods. Who could it be? Someone who knew the path. John? No, not unless he had closed The Club early, which was highly unlikely on a Friday night.

"Who goes there?"

"It's me, Kathy."

"What the hell are you doing out here in the dark?"

"Now that's a fine greeting."

"Sorry, I'm just surprised. Pleasantly I might add. It's been a while, how have you been?"

"Good, and you, Mick?"

"Okay, I guess."

"I brought you something," Kathy said.

"Come on in, I've got a good fire going. These fall nights get a little chilly. So what'd ya bring me?"

"At the risk of being presumptuous I brought you some camomile tea."

"Some what?"

"Camomile tea. It'll help you sleep, peacefully. I know you've got a problem with bad dreams, and you use alcohol to try and remedy that, but alcohol will only make you delirious in the long run, and you won't be able to distinguish between the dreams and reality."

"It's not that bad," Mick said.

"Not yet, maybe. Try the tea, Mick."

"Well, okay, let's have some now."

"Wait till you're ready to go to bed."

"I'm ready now, how about you?"

"No, Mick, we can't until you stop drinking." Kathy looked very serious. Her big blue eyes locked onto Mick's.

"Okay, I'll stop right now, I won't finish this bottle of beer."

"You'll just have another one after I leave."

"Then don't leave. Stay here all night. I could use the company."

"Have you been writing?" Kathy asked, abruptly changing the subject.

"Some."

"About Cambodia, and what's-her-name, Lovea?" There was a tinge of resentment in Kathy's tone.

"Yeah."

"I've been dying to know, Mick, was she your girlfriend over there?"

"No, just a friend. And this Reggie guy, is he your boyfriend?"

"How did you know about him?"

"I talked to him at the Phoenix House about post-traumatic stress, then I saw him with you one morning having breakfast at Mary Lou's Diner."

"We've dated some," Kathy said.

"I'm jealous," Mick said, and he meant it.

"Haven't you dated since we split up?" Kathy asked.

"If that's what you want to call it. This is the 70s, girl, people don't date anymore, they just have sex."

"Speak for yourself, Mick."

"Oh I am. I haven't had a real date since 1968."

"What do you call what we did?"

"Met in a bar, picked each other up."

"Well I'm glad you have such a high opinion of our relationship."

"We don't have a relationship any more. Remember, you walked out on me."

"I had to, Mick, I couldn't compromise my sobriety. Recovering alcoholics have to change playgrounds and playmates.

Maybe if you got sober we could teeter-totter again."

"Why do you make such a big deal out of me having a drink or two? It's not that I'm a falling-down drunk or anything like that."

"But I am, remember?"

"Yes. I do recall having to pick you up off the floor a time or two," Mick said.

"And if you recall, I kept you out of a fight or two in the bars when you got into arguments with peaceniks about the Vietnam War."

"Yes, and I remember that you were siding with them."

"The war was wrong, Mick, but let's not go over that old ground again. Let's have some of that tea, it'll relax us both."

They drank it by the hearth, with Mick in one stuffed chair and Kathy in another. Neither spoke another word. The warm, soft glow, and occasional crackling of the fire, and an owl hooting in the distance, caused Mick to drift off with Jazzpur the cat curled up in his lap, and Carmella the dog snoring at his feet. He awoke in the wee hours and Kathy was gone. He went to the loft and slept the rest of the night in peace, without the assistance of alcohol. The next day he went to Mr. Natural's Health Food Store in Carbondale and bought some bulk camomile.

In November, David called Mick to inform him that he hadn't won the Medal of Freedom. It was going to the popular, patriotic singer Kate Smith for her stirring renditions of "God Bless America."

America was in desperate need of God's blessing since the Vietnam War debacle, Watergate, and now an energy crisis and a failing economy marked by soaring inflation and a high rate of unemployment. Major American stalwart companies like Chrysler were on the verge of bankruptcy. In Detroit, unemployment figures reached 16.3 percent in late summer. Permanent plant closings announced by Ford added to the problem. Economists proclaimed, "...as Detroit goes so goes the nation."

America's woes in the late '70s and early '80s were not solely domestic. In November of '79 in Tehran a mob of 500 Iranian students, angered by our cozy relationship with the unpopular Shah of Iran, seized the United States Embassy and 90 hostages. In response, President Jimmy Carter froze the considerable Iranian assets in the U.S. and sent a naval task force to the Indian Ocean, where carrier-based jets and helicopters were within easy striking range of Iran.

Meanwhile, American television audiences were shocked to see blindfolded members of the United States Marines embassy guard, with their hands tied behind their backs were paraded before the cameras while the students chanted "Death to America, Death to Carter, Death to the Shah."

Effigies of Uncle Sam and Carter were burned, and scores of American flags were spat upon, trampled and burned in the street.

The U.S. sent mediators to Iran to seek the release of the hostages, but they had little success. The students, who had the support of Ayatollah Khomeini's government, continued to take a hard line, even though a trickle of hostages, mainly women and blacks were granted their freedom. Ultimately, fifty-two Americans remained in captivity. The deposed Shah, now gravely ill, had been hospitalized in the United States. It was his arrival in the U.S. that had set off the embassy attack, and the Iranian students demanded his return to Iran where he faced certain death.

To make matters worse, a U.S. military expedition to free the hostages met with disaster after a helicopter collided with a transport plane at a staging area in the Iranian desert. Eight Americans were killed, and several more were injured in the fiasco. After an early morning report at the White House on the failed mission, a stony-faced and haggard President Carter appeared on national television to tell the nation what had happened. He said he had ordered the cancellation of another operation in Iran that was under way, preparing for a rescue of the hostages. The mission was terminated because of equipment failure. During the subsequent withdrawal, there was another collision between aircraft on the ground at a remote desert location. Adding insult to injury, the Iranians celebrated the failures at a rally that was staged in front of the occupied American Embassy, and a broadcast from Tehran announced that the Iranians had defeated the Americans and their mercenaries, and forced them to retreat.

Chapter 35

In December, Mick took Lovea up on her offer to join her in testifying before the U.N. regarding Pol Pot's murderous rampage in Cambodia. Tired of flying all over the world, and for a change of pace, Mick took a bus to Chicago, then a train from Chicago to New York City. He arrived at Pennsylvania Station in midtown Manhattan surrounded by a plethora of skyscrapers. As he stood at the station's main entrance at West 32nd Street and 7th Avenue to hail a cab, the sky-piercing pinnacle of the Empire State Building came into view. Surpassed by Chicago's Sears Tower in height as the nation's tallest building, it still remained a world-renowned icon of New York City, along with the Statue of Liberty.

Riding up 7th Avenue to the Sheraton -- located between W.51st and 52nd Streets -- slowly because of the traffic, Mick caught a glimpse of Times Square, where Broadway diagonally intersects 7th Avenue at 45th Street. Down the block to his right, looking east on 49th, he saw the big Christmas tree at Rockefeller Center. Best of all, from his 21st floor room at the Sheraton he had a fantastic view of snowy Central Park.

The room had a refrigerator that offered adult beverages for a hefty price. Not hurting for money, Mick mixed a whiskey with Coke, put his feet up and took in the panorama of skyline and park. He had seen a lot of the world over the last couple of years, and it had left him in a perpetual state of jet lag. Even the long bus and train ride from Carbondale and Chicago to New York had made him tired and a little spacy, but the whiskey helped to perk him up, along with the new wave jazz playing on the radio. It all went beautifully with the view. The sun was going down, which cast a crimson glow over the snow of the park, and the lights of the city were coming on. He mixed another drink.

In the morning he'd contact Lovea; in the meantime he was enjoying the little party in his room. Mick didn't mind drinking alone. It was conducive to self-reflection and he liked what he saw, his image sipping whiskey, reflected on the glass of the window and superimposed over Manhattan's glittering skyline around the park, looking like an ad touting the good life in some slick magazine.

Ironic though, considering that one of the things about himself that concerned him most was his drinking. It had caused Kathy to leave him, but there were times when he couldn't sleep without the help of alcohol, especially when he started thinking about having killed Marcus Jackson. It was in self-defense he had always rationalized: Jackson had tried to kill him.

"I'll drink to that," he said toasting the reflection of himself on the window. By ten o'clock he had passed out on the bed.

The following afternoon, after a room service lunch, he went downstairs to ask if Lovea had checked in.

"Yes sir, she has."

"What's her room number?"

"I'm sorry, sir, that information is confidential, but I can ring her room for you, if you'd like."

"Please do."

"Hello." She answered the phone promptly.

"Lovea? It's Mick."

"Mick, where are you?"

"Here at the Sheraton, in the lobby. Can you meet me in the lounge in about twenty minutes?"

"Yes, of course. Looking forward to seeing you. Last time was in the jungle running for our lives."

"Yeah. I thought I'd never see you again," Mick said.

"Well, you will in twenty minutes," Lovea said.

Mick sat at a table in the lounge facing the door. In twenty minutes or so Lovea came in. Mick rose and they embraced, then they stood at arms length holding hands and they gave each other the once-over.

"You look different, Mick, with the gray streaks in your red hair, and the mustache; it becomes you."

"And your hair, Lovea, it's still so long and beautiful. And you're not so ungodly thin anymore. You look like you're in perfect shape."

"You too, Mick."

He had never thought of her in sexual terms. They were too busy trying to survive, and escape Phnom Penh to think about such things. He had always thought of her as sister-like. But now there seemed to be something else between them.

"Would you like a drink, Lovea?"

"Yes, a glass of wine would be fine, something white, *Tokay* perhaps, if they have it. It's Hungarian."

They had what she wanted and Mick got a beer.

"So, Lovea, when do you speak at the U.N.?"

"Tomorrow afternoon, but an Asian man, he looked Cambodian, brushed by me in the lobby this morning and passed me a note warning me not to. Obviously they are following me if they know what hotel I'm in."

"They?"

"The Khmer Rouge, of course. Mick, you've put your life in danger to help me before. I need your help once again. Since you've been a witness to atrocities, could you testify before the U.N.'s World Court? As a former correspondent for Voice of American, you have much credibility. Being an American in America the Khmer Rouge would not harm you, only me."

'What would they do?"

"Torture me, rape me, kill me. You know how brutal they can be."

"We should alert the police that you've been threatened," Mick said.

"What good would that do? They have their hands full already, protecting the citizens of New York. This is a foreign affair."

"You should stay in my room until you leave New York," Mick proposed. "In case they know what room you're in. They wouldn't know that we're connected until we go before the U.N. They'd have no reason to try to find out what room I'm staying in -- unless they're watching us now, of course."

Mick glanced about the lounge. It didn't appear that they were being watched. Only one other table was occupied, and the occupants weren't Asians.

"Excuse me a moment," Mick said.

He walked out into the lobby. He noticed a couple of Asians there. Japanese he thought, maybe Korean or Chinese, but they didn't appear to be Southeast Asians. He returned to Lovea.

"I'm in room 2102. I'll be waiting for you," Mick said.

They went their separate ways, each to their respective rooms. A short time later there was a knock on Mick's door. It was Lovea. She brought in a suitcase and leather satchel.

"Only one problem," she said smiling. "Who sleeps where?"

"Lady's choice," Mick said.

She sat on one side of the king size bed, then the other.

"This side's softest it seems. Do you mind?" she asked.

"Not at all."

Mick had planned to sleep on the floor. To his surprise, apparently he wouldn't have to, yet he felt shy about the proposed arrangement -- but Lovea wasn't shy about it at all. She stretched out and patted the bed next to her, subtly indicting she wanted Mick to lie down too, which he did, and she held his hand and told him that in Phnom Penh she had a crush on him.

"You were like that white knight in shining armor who came to rescue me. I wanted to make love with you," she confessed, "but the time wasn't right, with Khmer Rouge lurking about. Now they're here again. But let's not let that stop us now."

She put her arm across Mick's chest and kissed him on the nape of his neck. He turned his head and met her kisses as he unbuttoned her blouse, undid her bra, which conveniently fastened in front, and fondled her breasts while whispering in her ear.

"Let's take our clothes off."

She sat up in bed, took her blouse off, and slipped out of her slacks and hosiery while Mick undressed. They lay naked together caressing and kissing each other all over until they did what comes naturally for a man and a woman in that situation. He slipped into her, and she rose to meet him, arching her back while wrapping her legs around his hips, and the rhythm of their lovemaking reached a fever pitch as they came together in an oblivious state of ecstasy.

In the aftermath they lay side-by-side, spent from the intensity of the lovemaking.

"I knew you would be a wonderful lover, Mick," Lovea whispered.

"How could you tell?"

"It is in your eyes. They reveal passion when you look into mine."

"That's what I see when I look into yours," Mick said.

"I'm glad it's mutual. There is nothing more painful emotionally than unrequited love," Lovea said.

"Yeah, I experienced that in the fifth grade," Mick said, adding levity to the discussion. "I gave her a valentine and got nothing in return."

"I'm so sorry, Mick." She kissed him tenderly on the cheek. "So then, shall we attend to business?"

"Okay."

They dressed and Lovea went to the bathroom. When she came out she took papers from her satchel, and they sat at the desk.

"First of all," Lovea said, "I'll talk about the millions who have died at the hands of Pol Pot and the Khmer Rouge. That's when you'll come in as a witness, Mick. Tell them about the thousands of skulls and bones you saw piled high in the mass open graves at Kampong Cham, and the execution you witnessed at Takeo of the man who questioned the instructor re-educating the Capitalists relocated from the cities to think like Communists."

"And the man I saw shot at Kampong Luong working in the rice paddies who couldn't keep up, and sat down to rest," Mick added.

"Yes, then I'll protest Pol Pot being recognized by the United States as a representative of Cambodia at the U.N. It is a travesty for him to be regarded as such -- the murdering bastard. Besides, he is in exile. Since when do those in exile speak for their former country? And let's not forget, he was tried, convicted and sentenced to death by a court in absentia in Phnom Penh in 1979 for the mass murder of his countrymen."

"Where is he in exile?" Mick asked.

"Some say in the jungles of Thailand, others say China. He is a disciple of Mao you know, although he fashioned much of his agrarian revolution after old style, pre-Marxist Russian Communism when the peasantry, armed with plow and gun, as in China under Mao, emerged as a political force. Only in Cambodia, the peasantry was the Khmer Rouge."

"Speaking of old style, Lovea, I'm ready for another beer. It's nearly Happy Hour time."

"Happy Hour?"

"Drinks half price. We can eat the complimentary hors d'oeuvres for supper then go out on the town. I've always wanted to go to Studio 54, the disco, would you like to go?"

"What's a disco?"

"A place to dance, like in Saturday Night Fever with John Trivolta and the Bee Gees."

"Who are they?"

"American and Australian pop stars."

"I have not danced since re-opening the hotel," Lovea said. "It was a very festive night. We played records of Stephane Grappelli, have you heard of him?

"Yes, the French jazz violinist."

Lovea danced in a strange, but sensuous way, more at jazz than disco, and Mick's style was old fashioned rock n' roll -- a funky combination of the Jerk, the Hitchhike and the Swim. They stood out on the dance floor among those more hip, but they had a good time nonetheless, gyrating beneath the spinning crystal ball that reflected the multi-colored strobe lights directed on it, which caused them, along with the alcohol they had been drinking, to stagger back to their table where they laughed like children on a carnival ride. Lovea put her hand on Mick's.

"Let's go, before we get too drunk."

But it was too late. When they got back to the hotel, Mick passed out on the bed. He awoke in the morning with Lovea at the desk softly rehearsing her testimony out loud. Mick asked her to come back to bed.

"Not now, my sweet, I've got to concentrate on this."

"Aren't you hung over from drinking all that wine?" Mick asked.

"No, I'm French, remember?"

"Well I'm hung over; I need some breakfast. Let's go downstairs," Mick suggested.

"I need to shower first," Lovea said, "and dry my hair."

Mick washed up in the sink and brushed his teeth while Lovea showered, and after she dried her hair they went to the restaurant in the lobby. They ordered Belgiun waffles with sausage and orange juice and coffee.

"We're not far from Central Park. Let's go for a walk after we eat," Mick suggested.

"In these high heels? I'll need to go back up to the room and change shoes."

After they had finished breakfast and Lovea changed shoes, she and Mick walked up 5th Avenue to 59th Street to one of the entrances to Central Park where there was a gigantic bronze statue of General Sherman on a horse. Lovea marveled at it. "Who is he?" she asked.

"He was a hero in our civil war, like you are in yours. Someday there should be a statue of you in a park in Phnom Penh."

"My goodness, Mick. I am not of that stature."

"There is one of Joan of Arc in Paris. I liken you to her," Mick said.

"I would like to see that. I would like to see Paris, my father's home."

They walked around The Pond, which was frozen and fairly crowded with ice skaters, and to the Gapstow Bridge, and as they crossed it on the north end of The Pond, a man ran up behind them and stabbed Lovea in the back before they knew what was happening. Only when she fell forward, bleeding profusely from the wound, did Mick realize what had just happened. The man ran away and disappeared over the bridge. Lovea lay dying. Mick held her in his arms. Blood seeped from her mouth and nose. She tried to talk but could only manage a whisper.

"Tell this story."

An ambulance came but it was too late. Lovea had died.

The police came too. They asked Mick if he could identify the assailant. He couldn't. He had only seen him from the back as he ran away.

"Any idea who might want to kill her?" one of the cops in plain clothes asked.

"The Khmer Rouge," Mick said.

"Of Cambodia?"

"Yes. She was the leader of a counterinsurgency there, called the People's Republican Army who wreaked havoc with the Khmer Rouge. Most recently she was the leader of the People's Republican Party, an offshoot of the army and a faction of a coalition government in Cambodia. She was about to testify against the Khmer Rouge at the U.N. today."

The cop asked Mick if he knew of anyone from Cambodia in New York who could claim the body and have it flown back there.

"Not that I'm aware of. Those at the U.N. are sympathetic to Pol Pot, her mortal enemy. He is ultimately responsible for her death, I'm sure, having sent Khmer Rouge to track her down."

"Could you do it?" the cop asked. "Accompany her body back to Cambodia?"

Mick had no desire to return to that country, but there was no one else to see that she returned; otherwise she'd be buried in obscurity in New York City. She deserved a special funeral in Phnom Penh, and Mick would do what he could to see that she got it -- he hoped with the assistance of the Vietnamese General Vu Vo Ky, her dear friend and an officer in Vietnam's Cambodian puppet government, the People's Revolutionary Council.

Chapter 36

After arriving in Phnom Penh with Lovea's body -- the casket was kept in a room where baggage was being held for inspection -- Mick went directly to the Hotel Angkor knowing that Lovea's followers frequented it. Perhaps he'd run into General Ky there, to inform him of her murder. He was known to dine there, and it was about that time of day. Mick asked the maitre d' if he knew the General.

"Yes, that is he over there."

Mick approached his table.

"General Ky?"

"*Oui?*" He responded, apparently thinking Mick was French, and not expecting to encounter any Caucasians of other nationalities right then.

"I'm a friend of Lovea Duval."

"Yes, she's in New York City," the General said, recognizing that Mick spoke English.

"Not anymore, Sir."

"No?"

"No. She was murdered there, and I've brought her body back to Phnom Penh."

"Murdered? Oh no, how could this be! Who would...?"

"The Khmer Rouge," Mick said. "They didn't want her to testify against Pol Pot at the U.N. They stabbed her in the back while we were walking in Central Park."

"Yes, this is the cowardly way of the Khmer Rouge. Where is the body now?" the General asked.

"At the airport."

"We must bring it here. She shall lie in state in the lobby's rotunda. It is fitting; this was her home -- her palace if you will. Many will come through here to pay their respects. She was exalted, as you may know, as Cambodia's young matriarch of freedom, like her idol Joan of Arc."

"Yes I know."

The General enlisted the help of several of his soldiers to bring the casket in a truck from the airport to the hotel. Meanwhile, the news of her death was broadcast over Radio Phnom Penh, and the following day hundreds came through the hotel to view Lovea. They brought flowers to cover her casket, leaving only her face, set in a slight smile, exposed, looking so much like the moonlit stone faces of the beautiful celestial maiden figurines of her beloved Angkor Wat, befitting Mick thought, for a woman who would surely have her place someday in Cambodian lore.

Chapter 37

Mick returned to Carbondale, he hoped, for at least a couple of years. He wanted to settle down for a while and write his book. He finally had an ending, albeit a tragic one. Lovea Duval had died in his arms on a cold winter's day in New York City -- far away from her home. She had not lived long enough to see Cambodia completely free of the Khmer Rouge -- or free of the Vietnamese, who admittedly kept the former in check, along with Pol Pot whom they had banished to the jungle, but who incredibly continued to be recognized by the United Nations as its representative from Cambodia. Perhaps the last chapter hadn't been written after all, and couldn't be until this travesty was addressed. Mick had intended to do so by testifying at the U.N. along with Lovea against the murderous tyrant, but her untimely death had forestalled it. However, he could still testify in her stead. He had kept the testimony she had written. He could mail it in along with his accounts of the atrocities committed by the Khmer Rouge that he had personally witnessed. He had also witnessed Lovea's murder and, although he couldn't identify the killer, circumstances most definitely pointed to the Khmer Rouge. He'd get busy composing his testimony to supplement Lovea's.

In the meantime, though, Mick had immediate concerns to deal with on the home front, namely deflecting questions by the police about the disappearance of Marcus Jackson -- who hadn't disappeared entirely. One of his arms and his skull had surfaced over the last couple of years, and, most recently, a portion of his boat had washed ashore not far from Mick's house only two days after he had returned from New York.

How it had gone unseen in the lake for so long was a mystery to Mick. Surely boaters would have been seen it floating around, but apparently it had escaped detection, as had Mick. But the discovery of the skull by John had not escaped police attention, and they continued to search for answers in Jackson's disappearance.

There was also the unfinished business of Mick and Kathy's relationship. It was still in limbo but potentially salvageable if Mick quit drinking. There was also the matter of Reggie, the fellow councilor she was seeing. And Mick had recently been intimate with Lovea, raising the issue of fidelity if that would be a consideration for two people who had broken up, but who seemed to be holding out hope for reconciliation.

Kathy had made overtures by bringing Mick camomile tea to help him sleep, instead of relying on alcohol. As a result, Mick discovered that it worked, and he began to rely less and less on alcohol for self-medication -- but he continued to use it socially: going to The Club, occasionally Merlin's and P.K.'s, and at the house at Lake Wells when he invited people out to use the sauna, to fish and boat and swim, and otherwise just party in general. And while Mick enjoyed the socializing, he was at the same time very lonely, although Carmella and Jazzpur provided some company, it was not the sort of company he longed for. He wanted a lasting relationship with a woman with whom he could start a family. One who could accept his lifestyle. A woman who wouldn't mind living several miles from town, where at night wildcats and coyotes howled, and cottonmouth snakes were sometimes underfoot, like the cobras of Cambodia.

Cambodia was never too far from Mick's mind. It had been such an intimate part of his life recently. He kept up with what was going on there through newspapers and magazines. As Lovea had indicated in her letter, the country was at last on the road to recovery and perhaps on the verge of self-government, at least once the Vietnamese withdrew, although when they did there was the threat of the Khmer Rouge taking over again. They were still active, mostly along the border with Thailand, far away from Phnom Penh. They had managed to assassinate one of their rivals in Lovea, thereby eliminating any possibility that she would be selected to head a coalition government that would include Prince Sihanouk. International observers speculated this would come to pass when the Vietnamese withdrew under pressure from the U.N.

demanded the prompt withdrawal of all foreign forces -- like Vietnam -- from Cambodia. But the credibility of the U.N. suffered when the General Assembly voted overwhelmingly to allow the deposed Pol Pot to retain Cambodia's seat on the grounds that the invading occupation forces of Vietnam -- who now controlled the country through the puppet government of Heng Samrin, after ousting Pol Pot -- should not be rewarded for their aggression.

To further address the Cambodian problem, and acting on a resolution passed by the U.N.'s General Assembly, Secretary-General Kurt Waldheim convened a special conference in 1980 to seek a peaceful solution to the ongoing strife between the Vietnamese-installed government and the Chinese-backed Khmer Rouge. Two political groups participated, one loyal to Prince Sihanouk, and the other headed by his former premier Son Sann. No invitation was extended to the Heng Samrin regime, because it was considered by many, especially the U.S., to be illegitimate.

Waldheim's conference called for the withdrawal of all foreign forces, under the supervision of U.N. peace-keepers, and for free elections to be held under U.N. supervision. Representatives of the Sihanouk and Son Sann factions announced their intention to form a coalition government (which would have included Lovea Duval's People's Republican Party, had she lived) to oppose Vietnamese occupation of their country.

Despite making some headway regarding the Cambodian situation, the U.N. had only marginal impact on the maintenance of peace and security elsewhere, namely the invasion of Afghanistan by the Soviet Union (which led to the U.S. boycott of the Olympic Games in Moscow), the war between Iran and Iraq, and the tension between Arabs and Israelis.

Iran was not only in conflict with Iraq, but with the U.S. over the hostage taking of Americans in Tehran.

The United Nations actively sought the unconditional release of the hostages by sending Waldheim to Tehran to meet with the Ayatollah Khomeini in hopes of negotiating some kind of resolution. Waldheim failed, so the United States undertook several unilateral actions, including a break in diplomatic relations with Iran, the imposition of a trade embargo, and the abortive attempts to rescue the hostages, all of which failed to get results. The newly-elected Reagan Administration would finally free the hostages. Negotiations between the U.S. and Iran through Algerian intermediaries proved fruitful, and the 52 Americans held hostage since 1979 were released just minutes after Reagan was inaugurated in January of 1981.

Reagan's honeymoon was short-lived. A mere 70 days into his first term there was an attempt on his life.

On a rainy March afternoon in Washington D.C. a 25-year-old drifter named John Hinckley, Jr. fired several shots at the President's entourage with a .22-caliber pistol. A bullet ricocheted off the Presidential limo and entered Reagan's body below his armpit; it then bounced off one of his ribs and penetrated his lower left lung, coming to within an inch of his heart. A Secret Service agent, a D.C. cop and White House press secretary James Brady were also wounded -- Brady the most seriously; a bullet traveled through his brain, resulting in irreversible damage, but he lived, as did Reagan, who recuperated swiftly. Within a month the President was well enough to deliver a major address to a joint session of Congress on behalf of his bold new economic program, which was badly needed in the face of the severe recession inherited from the Carter Administration. The plan, which became known as Reaganomics, called for massive, long-term cuts in government spending and a 25% across-the-board cut in personal income taxes, which, it was hoped, would induce people to save, and in turn provide the capital to increase productivity, thus creating new jobs, lowering unemployment and reducing the rate of inflation.

Chapter 38

Assassination was the term Mick preferred to use in describing what he had done to Marcus Jackson -- not murder. It had been a political assassination of sorts, since the man had been the leader of Carbondale's Black Panthers. They were politically violent, like their ally the Weather Underground, who bombed buildings. The Black Panthers had shot it out with police nationwide, and Marcus Jackson, acting on behalf of the Weather Underground, had tried to kill Mick by bombing his house in Carbondale with a Molotov Cocktail. Live by the bomb, die by the bomb. Mick knew a bomb had been on board Jackson's boat because of the secondary explosion that occurred when Mick bombed it, but the police, to Mick's great relief, had concluded that the boat's gas tank had blown for some reason, perhaps as a result of a spark from a misfiring engine. The mechanic at the marina advanced a theory that such a scenario was possible. This was enough for the police, and they finally laid the case to rest.

But Mick wasn't about to put to rest Lovea's murder, which could also be characterized as a political assassination. There was no doubt about who was responsible, but the long arm of American law wouldn't reach Cambodia, which was way out of its jurisdiction, so justice would have to be carried out by the International Court of Justice -- also known as the World Court -- in the name of not only Lovea, but the millions of other Cambodians who were assassinated by Pol Pot's Khmer Rouge. Someone would have to speak for them.

Not being a lawyer, Mick would need help if he were to do it. He knew a lawyer in Springfield who specialized in international law -- Bill Panichi -- but would he be willing to help? Mick drove to Springfield to find out. He called him and they met at a tavern called the Cracked Crock, where, over a couple of beers Mick explained why he wanted to retain him. Bill responded very enthusiastically, having kept up with what was happening in Cambodia. He too was appalled that Pol Pot had thus far escaped justice.

Bill was a short, bearded man who stood tall in the law community of the town that had produced the nation's most famous lawyer, Abraham Lincoln. Like Lincoln, Panichi did a substantial amount of pro bono work. At the same time, he represented well-to-do international clients like Caterpillar of nearby Peoria, and Archer Daniels Midland of neighboring Decatur.

"International criminal law would be an entirely different story though, Mick," Bill said. "I'd have to consult my library, starting with accounts of the Nuremberg Trials to see if there are any precedents on which I could base a case. This would be an expensive proposition, Mick, and it would entail my going to New York at least once."

"Yeah, I know. I could pay you a retainer and the balance in installments, if that would be okay."

"Sure. How about a thousand dollars up front and we'll figure out the rest out as we go. Give me a day or two to research Nuremberg, then we'll go from there," Bill said.

"Great, we'll stay in touch. I'm staying at the Holiday Inn. I'll be there for two more nights."

"All right, I'll call you there tomorrow afternoon."

From the Cracked Crock, after he and Bill parted, Mick paid a visit to one of his old haunts, the infamous Office Tavern, an Italian joint that specialized in pizzas. He ordered a small pizza and a glass of Pabst Blue Ribbon beer, the house draft.

The place was still run by the DiLellos -- Mama in the kitchen and Tommy behind the bar. Tommy seemed glad to see Mick; it had been about four years since he had been there. They shook hands. The place was crowded and Mick looked around to see if he knew anybody, and right away he spotted Marty Grady, who at 6' 5" with his familiar tuft of blond hair, stood out above the crowd. It had been a while since Mick had seen him. Marty was in and out of town a lot. He was footloose and fancy free, literally. He often walked about barefoot, when the weather was warm. Hippies had nothing on him; they wore sandals. Mick went over to Marty and looked down at his feet; they were bare except for a bandage on his big toe.

"Stepped on broken glass in the river," he explained.

It was Marty who had taught Mick to fish with his bare hands, a skill he found useful while lost in the jungle in Cambodia.

"Where have you been, Mick, it's been a while."

"Carbondale mostly." Mick didn't care to get into the details of his trek through Southeast Asia right now; maybe later.

"And you, Marty?"

"California, Arizona, Texas, Michigan, Wisconsin."

"Doing what?" Mick asked.

"I sell gems to jewelry makers."

"Where do you get those?"

"Burma mostly."

"You've been there too?"

"Oh yeah, I forgot to mention that."

"Me too," Mick said.

"What, you were in Burma?" Marty asked with surprise.

"Rangoon." Mick had opened the proverbial can of worms. He now felt compelled to explain why he had been there, thinking that Marty would be intrigued, but he wasn't impressed. Marty contended that the U.S., particularly the CIA, meddled too much in foreign affairs, as in Vietnam.

Mick argued that the world needed to hear what the Khmer Rouge were doing in Cambodia.

"Tell the world about what good ole Uncle Sam is doing in El Salvador and Nicaragua!" Marty, who was never shy about expressing himself, got a little red-faced. His eyes looked angry.

"What's he doing?" Mick asked.

"Interfering with the revolutions there because we're afraid the Communists will prevail, just like we did in Vietnam."

"But aren't the Cubans and Soviets providing military aid to El Salvador through Nicaraguan to support the Marxist insurgents who are trying to overthrow President Duarte simply because he's pro-U.S."

"Yeah, and just like in Vietnam when we propped up Theiu, we're propping up Duarte just because he's anti-Communist," Marty argued.

No doubt Marty was well-read (despite being a high school dropout who later got a GED while in the Navy) and Mick couldn't argue about what he didn't know.   He recalled how arguments between the two had sometimes got out of hand, especially when they were drinking, so he changed the subject by inviting Marty down to Lake Wells. He'd be impressed with Mick living in the woods in a stone house, being a disciple of Henry David Thoreau he remembered. But Marty changed the subject back to Cambodia.

"I've got a book you should read called *U.S. Relations with Cambodia Under Jimmy Carter.* Next time you're in town come by the house, I'll give it to you."

Chapter 39

The following afternoon Mick got a call at the motel from Bill about what he had discovered about precedents set forth at Nuremberg for trying war criminals -- information that could be used to try Pol Pot before the World Court.

"The Allies' decision to indict the Nazi leaders at Nuremberg definitely had a precedence. Article 227 of the 1919 Treaty of Versailles called for the trial of major German war criminals, with the Kaiser at the top of the list. At Nuremberg, the Germans were to be judged for behavior involving the treatment of civilians, murder, abuse, deportation, slave labor, the murder of prisoners of war, the killing of hostages, plunder of public and private property, and the wanton destruction of cities and towns and villages, all of which comprised the genocidal destruction of European Jews. This is similar to the behavior of the Khmer Rouge under Pol Pot in their genocidal reign of terror in Cambodia.

"The American prosecutor at Nuremberg said, in a nutshell, they were establishing procedures for the future. History will make no distinction between the Nazi war criminals and genocidal tyrants of the future, he said. Therefore a precedent has been set for the prosecution of war crimes, and crimes against humanity under the World Court's global jurisdiction that would apply in prosecuting Pol Pot and the Khmer Rouge. So, Mick, we can precede with the precedent set at Nuremberg."

"What's the next step?" Mick asked.

"Can we get eyewitnesses to the atrocities, besides yourself of course, to come to New York to testify?"

"I can think of one in particular who was a prisoner of the Khmer Rouge, Ing Pech. He is living in Phnom Penh. I saw him at Lovea's funeral. He stays at the Hotel Angkor. I'll write him and ask if he can find other witnesses to come with him to New York."

"They would need to come to Springfield first, to discuss their role in this, before we go on to New York," Bill said. "Meanwhile, can you provide me with the tapes you recorded for Voice of America, along with the testimony Lovea was going to present to the World Court before she was murdered?"

"I'll contact Voice of America for the tapes. I've got Lovea's testimony."

"Okay, now call me if you hear back from this Ing Pech guy. You say he was a prisoner of war?"

"Yeah, at Tuol Sleng, the worst of all prisons anywhere. Sixteen thousand prisoners were executed there after prolonged torture that sometimes entailed attaching electrified prongs to their tongues and genitalia, Ing said. He told me that nearly all the prisoners signed coerced confessions that they worked as agents for the U.S., the Soviets and the Vietnamese.

"'Without a signed confession,'" an interrogation officer told Ing, 'we won't let you die easily.'"

"The torture and execution of political prisoners of war was one of the transgressions of which the Nazis at Nuremberg were convicted," Bill said. "Again, we've got a precedent to use."

Chapter 40

Back at Lake Wells Mick wrote to Voice of America to get copies of his tapes on the atrocities. He wrote to Ing in Phnom Penh to persuade him to come to Springfield to help prepare a case against Pol Pot, and urged Ing to find other witnesses to testify.

Ing wrote back immediately saying that he'd come to the U.S., in a sampan if necessary, and that he would try to round up other witnesses. One in particular that he had in mind was a bulldozer operator who, because of his experience in road construction pre-Pol Pot, had shoveled dirt on mass graves, *"burying thousands who had perished as anonymously as so many swine in a slaughter house. At least at Auschwitz they had numbers.*

"Realistically though, Mick, I can't afford to go all the way to this Springfield, Illinois. Where is it? I know Los Angeles, California where many Cambodians have gone. How far from there to Springfield?"

Ing's mentioning Cambodian exiles in California gave Mick an idea. He could fly Ing and the bulldozer operator to Los Angeles, where they could recruit others to come to New York via Springfield to testify about atrocities before the World Court. Along with tickets for the flight from Phnom Penh to L.A. he'd send enough money for Ing to reserve an entire train car for select exiles.

Mick ran the idea past Bill.

"Go for it," he said.

So Mick wrote Ing again about his plan, and with the letter he included two plane tickets usable at any time within the next three months, along with enough cash to reserve a train car in LA for the Cambodians. Ing wrote back that he was sure he could recruit many of his countrymen to testify.

"I'll call you when I get to Los Angeles," he said.

Bill liked the idea of Cambodians testifying en masse, reflective of the masses who had suffered under Pol Pot.

"Only problem is, they'll suffer even more having to sleep on that damn train," Bill said, "from LA to New York and back again."

"That's a price I'll bet they'll be willing to pay, though, if we can get the World Court to convene a tribunal to prosecute Pol Pot," Mick was sure.

Chapter 41

On one of Mick's frequent trips to Springfield to work with Bill on the appeal for a tribunal, he went to Marty's mother's house (where Marty stayed when he was in town) to get the book on *U.S. Relations with Cambodia Under Jimmy Carter.*

"Marty, since you've read the book maybe you can tell me why the U.S. voted yes to have Pol Pot represent Cambodia at the U.N."

"Oh, that's pretty simple, really. It all boils down to a political chess game between China, us and the U.S.S.R. with Cambodia and Vietnam as the pawns. Vietnam is backed by the Soviets and the Khmer Rouge by the Chinese. We tried to attain full diplomatic relations with China at the expense of relations with their chief rival in the region, the Soviets. Our anti-Vietnam/Soviet, pro-China stance led to the condemnation of Vietnam's invasion of Cambodia without considering the plight of Cambodians, should the Vietnamese leave the country to the Khmer Rouge. And while the Chinese and the Khmer Rouge have deplorable human rights records, the Carter administration, which always professed to be concerned about such matters, has the audacity to support them regardless.

"Shit, Man, I mean we voted yes to have the Khmer Rouge speak for Cambodia at the U.N. simply because we objected to Vietnam's invasion of Cambodia, and their propping up a puppet regime, which the U.S. considers an illegitimate successor to Pol Pot despite his murderous ways. And secondly we didn't want to alienate our new-found friend the Chinese, a supporter of the Khmer Rouge, regardless of their human rights record. Talk about hypocrisy, Man, just because we're anti-Vietnamese."

"I'm definitely against Vietnamese expansionism too, Marty. I participated in a war that was fought to prevent it, you know, the

Domino Theory, but there's no way I can support the Khmer Rouge after having seen first hand what they're capable of. I guess that's the diplomatic dilemma we face in choosing sides, and incredibly we've chosen the Khmer Rouge. To hell with human rights. Well, Marty, I guess I won't have to read the book now since you've told me all about it."

"Read it anyway, Mick, I haven't told you everything."

"Okay. And remember, you've got a standing invitation to visit me down at Lake Wells. Go to Carbondale first and call me for directions. Here's my number."

"See ya, Mick."

"So long."

But it wasn't that long. As soon as Mick got back to Lake Wells he got a call from Marty.

"I'm in Carbondale, how do I get to your place?"

Mick gave him directions. He knew Marty could easily follow them even though they were rather involved especially through the woods from the county road to the house. No problem, Marty had the instincts of an Indian scout; in an hour he showed up with a backpack and sleeping bag, a bottle of wine and an ounce of weed.

"Wow!" he said when he looked around the inside of the round stone house. "Love the loft, and that stained glass skylight. And the double-hearth fireplace right up the middle. Man, you built this place?"

"With a lot of help from my friend John. He was a Sea Bee. He owns The Club in town. I'll introduce you when we go in. Meanwhile let's have some of that wine. We'll take it down to the water. It's about time for the sunset. It's beautiful here," Mick said.

"This whole scene is beautiful. How did you find this place?" Marty asked.

"Newspaper."

"Lucky man."

"Yeah, it went down to me bidding for the land against some hippie chick from Carbondale. I ended up selling her two acres of the ten I bought. She lived out here for awhile in a teepee with her boyfriend, but she got pregnant and had to move back to town."

"Oh, makin' whoopee in the wigwam, eh?"

The weed Marty brought went well with the wine, providing a sweet, smoky taste to the palate, like smoking a rum-soaked cigar, the difference being the high derived from the marijuana which enhanced the experience of observing the rippling reflection of the setting sun on the deep green waters of the lake.

Marty had rolled a gigantic joint, and between that and the bottle of wine they passed back and forth, they were getting good and stoned.

As the sunset faded into twilight, stars began to appear, growing brighter as the sky grew darker -- suns every one, many much larger than ours.

"I wonder how many Earth-like planets revolve around those stars," Marty pondered aloud, sensing (as he was known for his extra-sensory perception) that's what Mick was observing.

"Probably millions, given how vast the universe is," Mick said.

"Well then here's a question to consider. Do they believe in the same God Earthlings do?"

"That would depend on whether or not they're aware of the Bible and the Book of Genesis in the Old Testament in which God is credited with creating the universe, and man in the Garden of Eden," Mick said.

"So if they're aware of the Book of Genesis in which God is the originator of the cosmos and the creator of the Garden of Eden, the birthplace of man, then it would follow that men elsewhere are the sons of God who believe in Him," Marty postulated.

"If you so conclude," Mick said.

"But there's one thing that puzzles me about the story of the Garden of Eden. Why did God tempt Adam and Eve by planting a tree of forbidden fruit. Sounds like entrapment to me," Marty said.

"He wanted to give man the option of choosing between obedience to God or disobedience, as in sin. Adam and Eve chose disobedience at the urging of Satan disguised as a serpent. That was the original sin," Mick said.

"So in a way God's an existentialist in that he's given us the option of free will as opposed to divine destiny. But it sounds like an experiment that went awry, testing man to see of he was obedient to God or Satan.

Obviously it's the latter. I mean, hell, look what's going on all over the world – wars, and mass murder in Cambodia. And what happened to the sacrifice his other son Jesus made for the atonement of our sins?"

"That's gone awry too, I'm afraid," Mick said.

"Speakin' of sin, let's go in to town and see if we can pick up a couple of those Carbondale hippie chicks you were talking about," Marty said, ever the chauvinist pig.

"We'll go to The Club first. I'll introduce you to John. Then we can go across the street to Merlin's. A lot of chicks go in there on Friday nights," Mick said, ever the chauvinist pig. "Better put on some shoes though. You know, no shoes, no shirt, no service."

Marty got a pair of sandals from his backpack, and they drove to town in his Chevy van -- about a ten mile trip. First they went to The Club where Mick introduced Marty to John.

"Understand you were in the Navy," Marty said.

"Yep."

"Me too."

"Oh yeah, where were you stationed?" John asked.

"On the Pueblo. No, just kidding. A year at Great Lakes and three in San Francisco. Never left shore."

"Dry dock, huh?"

"More like dry dick," Marty said. "That town is hard to score in if you're not a faggot."

"Carbondale should be easier if that's what you're looking for," John said. "Not so much action in here though, to be honest, being as it's a vet bar."

"Yeah, thought we'd go over to Merlin's," Mick said, remembering that he had met Alice there after he had come back from his second stint in Vietnam.

They had a beer with John then went across the street. A band was playing, and Marty and Mick stood off to the side with their drinks and watched the women dance. One of them, to Mick's pleasant surprise, was Alice, dancing with a girlfriend. Women did that. If a man danced with his boyfriend it'd be an entirely different story. At any rate, when Alice and her friend finished, Mick approached them.

"Remember me?" he asked.

"Sure do, Mick. How have you been?"

"Fine."

"This is Jill." Alice introduced her friend who was tall like Marty.

"And this is Marty, may we join you?" Mick asked.

"Yeah, we're sitting at a table over there."

They all sat down.

"I was hoping to see you here again, Alice," Mick said.

"I'm in here every Friday night. It took you long enough to come back," she said.

"Yeah, well, I've been out of town a lot."

"If I remember, don't you live out at Lake Wells?"

"Sure do. Wanna go out there and use the sauna?" Mick asked.

"What d'ya say, Jill?" she asked her friend.

"Sounds great, let's go."

"Where're ya parked?" Mick asked.

"Out front."

"So are we. Follow us. It's about ten miles."

"Wow, that was fast," Marty said when they got in the van.

"Alice is fast," Mick said bluntly.

"Hope Jill is too."

"Birds of a feather, Marty."

When they got to where Mick always parked before walking through the woods to the house, he held Alice's hand and led the way. There was enough moonlight by which to see, and it cast beautiful rippling reflections on the lake.

"Oh, let's go for a midnight swim!" Alice shouted.

"I thought we came out here to sauna," Jill said.

"First things first," Mick said. I've got a bottle of Jack that needs to be drunk, then we'll sauna and swim."

They went to the house and Mick mixed the whiskey with Coke in glasses with ice. Marty declined, saying he'd had enough to drink, which would prove fortuitous.

After the wine Mick had drunk, and the beers he'd had at The Club and Merlin's, he got pretty high on one glass of Jack and Coke, in fact he got drunk. And so did the women.

"Time to sauna." Mick took off his clothes and Marty followed. The women were initially hesitant, but they soon did the same.

After getting naked and hot and sweaty in the sauna, they jumped in the lake to cool off, splashing about and dunking each other like kids. In the mayhem, Alice disappeared under the water, unnoticed by the others at first, then Jill screamed,

"Where's Alice!"

Marty went under to try to find her. Mick tried to help, but he was too drunk. He thrashed about and swallowed water, and was choking as he floundered and struggled to stay afloat. Marty dove down here and there and finally he found Alice lying unconscious on the bottom. He pulled her up, towed her to shore, and tried to resuscitate her by repeatedly pressing on her back to pump water out of her lungs. Soon she threw up and began to breathe. Mick stood by helplessly. He was ashamed that he was too drunk to help save Alice. If it hadn't been for Marty, she would have drowned. It was a close call and a very sobering experience, literally: after that, Mick quit drinking in earnest, and went to Kathy to tell her what had happened, and that he was going to sober up.

"Don't think in terms of forever. Just take it one day at a time."

Mick had heard the cliche' before, but it was one of the tenets of AA that worked, according to those who had been sober for years, one day at a time.

Kathy had been sober for nearly four years, so she knew what she was talking about. And she suggested Mick attend AA on a regular basis to bolster his sobriety with tried and true philosophy.

He particularly liked Steps 2,3, and 11. Two: that we have come to believe that a Power greater than ourselves can help us get sober. Three: that we decide to turn our will and our lives over to the care of God as we understand Him. And 11: that we seek through prayer and meditation to improve our conscious contact with God as we understand Him, praying only for knowledge of His will for us, and the power to carry that out. In other words, we call upon a Higher Power as we understand it to help guide us.

Mick recalled distinctly how he had summoned his higher power to save him when he was trapped between two boulders in the jungle in Cambodia, and when he was held captive by the Khmer Rouge. He would surely have died there if not for divine intervention, but he had grown complacent about it once he was free and living the good life back home.

Chapter 42

Mick and Kathy attended the same AA meetings. When they stood up in a circle holding hands with the other drunks while reciting the Lord's Prayer at the close of the meetings, they began to bond again.

After four months of attending meetings twice a week with Mick, Kathy broke up with Reggie and moved in with Mick again. They were careful not to make the same mistake they had made early in their previous relationship -- an unwanted pregnancy which resulted in an abortion, but because of what must have been a leaky diaphragm, Kathy became pregnant again. This time they agreed to have the baby because they both wanted to start a family -- but not without being married. They married in a simple ceremony, overseen by a recovering alcoholic they knew from AA, who happened to be a minister.

They didn't take a honeymoon. Living at Lake Wells was special enough, especially in early spring before it became ungodly hot. But Mick wouldn't be spending much of the summer at home. He went back and forth to Springfield throughout May, June and July working with Bill to prepare a case on behalf of the Cambodians from LA who would go to New York to protest Pol Pot being a spokesman for them at the U.N., and to see that he was tried for war crimes before the World Court.

The Cambodians, along with Ing Pech, came through Springfield on the train en route to New York on August 10. Mick and Bill boarded the train and greeted the contingent who occupied one entire car. Ing, a highly educated man in his own right, had selected educated Cambodians who spoke English, for this endeavor. Many of those who fled Cambodia for California were educators and professionals. They had been targeted for death or imprisonment by the Khmer Rouge before escaping in the nick of time. Many of their colleagues didn't make it. To this they would testify at the U.N.

It had been a long trip from LA to Springfield -- two days -- and it would take another day to reach New York City. They had brought food for themselves that wouldn't readily spoil: spring rolls, won tons, hard boiled eggs, and thermoses of tea which they offered to share with Mick and Bill. The two Illinoisans opted for coffee in the club car where they went with Ing to discuss how they'd go about addressing the court with so many witnesses.

"Out of the group we'll call only three to testify, Ing. Any more and it would be redundant. The very presence of the others will suffice as a show of force. In addition, we'll be playing Mick's Voice of America tapes and I'll have Mick read the testimony Lovea Duval composed. That should be enough to convince the court to convene a tribunal, especially since Pol Pot has already been tried and convicted for mass murder in Cambodia" Bill said.

"Very well. I trust in your judgement," Ing said.

As the train rolled slowly away from the station and gradually picked up speed after leaving the lazy little city of Springfield, Ing remarked on how orderly and peaceful train travel was in the U.S.

"In Cambodia many people ride on top of the train because it gets so crowded inside. And rail travel is very dangerous, especially in the west of Cambodia near Thailand where Khmer Rouge guerrillas lurk. Two railway cars are run in front of the engine and are weighted with rails and spare wheels to set off mines along the tracks. Interspersed among the passenger cars are the ones with armor plates and machine guns, manned by Vietnamese soldiers to fend off ambushes by the Khmer Rouge. Here in America the conductor is the only man in uniform that we see on the train, besides an occasional G.I. Wish someday there would be G.I.s in Cambodia to keep the peace."

"G.I.s were there during the Vietnam War in 1970," Bill said. "It brought anything but peace. In America there was widespread dissent over what many considered to be an invasion of Cambodia accompanied by relentless bombing. It reached a flashpoint at Kent State University in Ohio where protesting students were shot dead by National Guardsmen."

"I thought only in Cambodia did soldiers kill their own citizens," Ing said.

"No," Bill said bluntly.   He was an old peacenik who had been outspoken about the war himself as a student at the University of Illinois.

"True to history, Bill, it's important to point out that the so-called invasion of Cambodia was undertaken to rid the country of North Vietnamese Army and Viet Cong sanctuaries that had been established there in violation of the Geneva Accords of 1954," Mick said.   "It was the Vietnamese Communists who widened the war beyond South Vietnam's border."

"Ironic isn't it," Ing said, "that it's the Vietnamese who are the peace keepers in Cambodia now."

"How do you feel, Ing, about the Vietnamese being your protector against the Khmer Rouge?" Bill asked.

"Very troubling, but I believe things will change soon when a Cambodian-based coalition government is formed.   Unfortunately it may include an element of the Khmer Rouge, which is troubling also, when one considers what they have done to the people of Cambodia. But the world, for the most part, has chosen to ignore it because they consider the Khmer Rouge to be the legitimate government of Cambodia because it ruled the country from 1975 until 1979 when the Vietnamese invaded.   Apparently they see Khmer Rouge atrocities to be the lesser of the two evils compared to Vietnamese expansionism. It is a dilemma the Cambodian people have been forced to face.

"But I believe it could be resolved if the coalition is led by Prince Sihanouk, who has organized the National United Front for an Independent, Neutral, Peaceful and Cooperative Cambodia. Sihanouk's group, along with the newly-formed People's National Liberation Front -- an offspring of Lovea Duval's People's Republican Army and Party -- headed by Son Sann, comprises the Non-Communist Resistance. Together these forces would neutralize the Communist Khmer Rouge and give balance to the coalition, which is being called Democratic Kampuchea.   It is all that stands in the way of Vietnam permanently occupying the country -- and their aggression has gone far beyond our borders.   In April the Vietnamese pursued Cambodian Non-

Communist Resistance troops into Thailand, where they engaged Thai forces in sustained combat, leaving little doubt that their aggression is limitless."

"So, am I to conclude that in opposition to the Vietnamese occupation you are willing to accept the Khmer Rouge as part of a coalition government?" Bill asked.

"Only if they are kept in check by the other factions, and not allowed to impose the brutal policies that were forced on the people during the Pol Pot years. Under the new leadership of Khieu Samphan, a moderate, I believe they will conduct themselves in a civilized manner. Meanwhile Pol Pot must answer for the crimes he committed when ruling the Khmer Rouge in the past."

"By the way, Mick," Bill said, "yesterday I checked with the New York City police and the FBI to see if they had any leads regarding the murder of Lovea. They said they found a knife in the shallows of The Pond that they thought might be the murder weapon, but all the finger prints had been washed away, of course. Then they tried to question Cambodian officials at the U.N. -- who declared diplomatic immunity, which allowed questioning to go no further, basically, than what is your name and title."

"It makes you wonder what they've got to hide," Mick said.

"Oh, these are Khmer Rouge," Ing said. "Very experienced in murder. All are guilty if only one killed Lovea. What do you call it? Complicity."

"Yes, if we can get Pol Pot tried for war crimes many of his Khmer Rouge henchmen will go on trial too, like the Nazi conspirators at Nuremberg," Bill said. "Lovea's murder would fall under a blanket indictment for the murder of all Cambodians en masse."

"Very well then," Ing said. "Let us proceed."

Chapter 43

When they arrived in New York Ing wanted to see where Lovea died and place a small wreath of flowers at the site, so Mick hailed a cab and they stopped at a florist on the way to Central Park. Bill and the others went on to the U.N. In two hours they were scheduled to go before the World Court. They'd meet again at that time.

Mick and Ing entered the park near the majestic statue of Sherman on his mount, and they followed the walk around The Pond onto Gapstow Bridge.

"It was here that she was stabbed in the back." Mick looked down and was surprised to see that faint blood stains remained in the concrete.

Ing laid the wreath on the ground. People would walk around it, or someone would pick it up unaware that on this bridge over The Pond a legend had ended, half way around the world from where it began in the dark and dank cellar of a hotel in Phnom Penh.

Having paid their respects, Mick and Ing took a cab to the U.N. where they met with Bill and the exiles in the lobby before going up to the confines of the World Court where, after exhaustive formalities of protocol, Bill addressed the court. While he was in the habit of speaking rather softly in casual conversation, Bill became very forceful before the court.

"Since 1975 when Pol Pot and the Khmer Rouge conquered Cambodia, an estimated two to three million people, of a population of seven and a half million, have perished as a result of overwork, starvation, torture and execution.

"With us today are representatives of the survivors, who come before you to urge the convening of a tribunal to prosecute and punish those who were responsible for this unconscionable reign of terror.

"I stand humbly before you now, in the stead of the irreplaceable Lovea Duval, former leader of Cambodia's People's Republican Army and Party. She was scheduled to speak before you last December, but was murdered by an unknown assailant in Central Park. Her words live on." Bill read them.

"*Under the bloody reign of Pol Pot, millions were murdered by his Khmer Rouge, summarily executed simply for being too bourgeois for the Communists' liking. He liquidated the middle class, seizing all private property, and depopulated the cities, sending the inhabitants to what amounted to concentration camps in the countryside to fulfill his dream of creating an agrarian utopia, but it resulted in a nightmare for Cambodia.*

"*Many suffered prolonged torture before dying, others starved or were worked so hard they died.*

"*Pol Pot committed the genocide of his own people, yet the United Nation's General Assembly has voted to recognize him as the voice of Cambodia, while the voices of the people were condemned to silence in mass graves.*

"*Why should this monster continue to be heard, moreover, why should he continue to be free. He must be brought to justice before an international court of law for the crimes he has committed against humanity. Let his voice be heard hear in defense of his murderous legacy. Let it be his Nuremberg.*"

Bill continued with his own testimony. "There is little doubt that Lovea Duval's killing was a political assassination perpetrated by the long, lethal arm of the Khmer Rouge whose murderous ways know no bounds. The United Nations should also know no bounds in holding violators of human rights under international law accountable for their actions before this honorable court, which was established for that very purpose. I know of no circumstances the world over that merits a tribunal more than what has occurred over the last seven years in Cambodia. The precedent was set at Nuremberg 36 years ago, as I'm sure this learned court knows. What's more, Pol Pot has already been convicted for mass murder in Phnom Penh. This in itself should suffice as a precedent for the World Court to follow in convicting him again, once and for all.

"But, with all due respect, the U.N.'s disdain for Vietnam's invasion of Cambodia seems to take precedence over the Khmer Rouge's blatant violation of human rights. Although the invasion is also a violation of international law, it has resulted in the ending of genocide in Cambodia. To this end, all else is secondary in comparison. In due time, the Vietnamese will withdraw. Will Pol Pot then be free to resume his murderous ways? We cannot afford to wait and see. There is sufficient evidence to prosecute now, and the Cambodians who have come before you today can bear witness. Through their eyes, through their tears, they have seen the results of his madness. They have seen their loved ones dragged away to be executed or imprisoned simply because they were deemed to be too bourgeois, too educated, too urbanized to fit into the Khmer Rouge's plans for an agrarian utopia, so they were eliminated.

"But elimination does not adequately describe the horror of it all. Chan Mith, a bulldozer operator at one of the death camps will tell you in very graphic terms what he observed from the seat of his bulldozer."

"Bloated from the sun and stiff from rigor mortis, the piles of bodies did not settle well when shoveled into the shallow mass graves. Limbs, including skulls, protruded above the surface of the dirt, and were swarming with flies. It was a nightmarish landscape that visits me when I sleep."

Muffled sobbing could be heard among the Cambodians reliving the final, grotesque demise of some of their loved ones. One woman among them spoke.

"My husband, a physician and the father of our three children, was taken from us in 1975 before the children and I were forced into a re-education camp. Now, seven years later I learn of his dreadful fate. This is the fate of millions who perished simply because they were educated. Pol Pot spoke of an agrarian utopia. His propagandists drummed this into our brains at the camps at night after we toiled in the paddies all day, yet the people starved. They talked about Cambodia becoming an economic leader among the nations of Southeast Asia, yet they closed the factories, murdered entrepreneurs, eliminated the middle class and abolished our money, the riel. Pol Pot has destroyed Cambodia; he must be punished."

There was an uproarious response among the exiles, who had until now been patient and respectfully quiet. Then Bill introduced Mick.

"Also with us today is Mick Scott, who while posing as a reporter for Radio Moscow lauding the Khmer Rouge's agricultural revolution, actually filed reports for Voice of America to expose the true nature of this bloody revolution to the world."

Mick stood and positioned his tape recorder so that it could be heard over the PA microphone.

In the middle of the night in the secrecy of a dark room in an abandoned hotel in deserted Phnom Penh, my guide, who like me was posing as a Communist while working for Voice of America, quietly spoke of the schism that had developed between two groups of Cambodian society as a result of Pol Pot's revolution.

There were the so-called Old People, which comprised the rural, rice-growing peasants who identified closely with the Khmer Rouge because they also came from the countryside. And there were the New People who had been expelled from the cities and towns. They were considered to be the enemy that was in need of rehabilitation. They had comprised the bourgeois middle-class who didn't share Pol Pot's dream of an agrarian utopia for Cambodia. Their accustomed lifestyles would only get in the way of it, and sap the revolution of its esprit de corps by being materialistic like societies of the hated West.

Under the Khmer Rouge, the New People were no longer allowed to own anything, not even a cooking pot. Their families were separated – the men and women and children had to live apart in communal long houses where they were forced to sleep with strangers in filthy, 45-foot collective beds after working 18 hours a day plowing, hoeing or building irrigation works on pitiful rations of maggot-infested rice gruel. If they were too weak in the morning to work, and asked to be excused the cadre' would say, "Ah, while we suffered in the forest to liberate the country, you were lazy and comfortable in Phnom Penh. Now you must work!"

At night the New People were forced to meet and criticize each other in front of the cadre' about what they may have done wrong that day, like slacking off, or picking up anything to eat – a piece of fruit, a root, a worm. If they were criticized two or three times, they were killed.

There were racks of steel bars for breaking necks, and shallow, electrified pools through which malcontents were forced to wade at gun point. If they tried to get out they risked being shot. It depended on the whim of the cadre' who lorded over them with the power of life or death. More often than not they chose the latter.

From deep inside the broken heart of Cambodia this is Mick Scott reporting.

Bill addressed the court again, ever-so-briefly, because all that could be said had been said.

"In closing, I plead with this honorable court to convene a tribunal and bring this tyrant, Pol Pot, and his henchmen to justice."

The contingent, led by Ing Pech, then filed out to a waiting bus. They were driven directly to Penn Station where they boarded the train for their return trip to LA via Springfield, satisfied, at least for the time being, that they had had their day in court. They hoped there'd be many more if the court voted in favor of trying Pol Pot.

Chapter 44

About a month after the Cambodian contingent spoke before the World Court, Mick and Bill received a letter from Ing Pech. He had stayed in Los Angeles because the Vietnamese-installed Heng Samrin government now prohibited non-Communist Cambodians from returning to the country.

"*They have tightened their grip on the population of Cambodia," he wrote. They have curtailed freedom of religion and freedom of movement. But the three principal resistance groups of the new coalition government, the Communist Khmer Rouge, the non-Communist Khmer People's National Liberation Front (formerly Lovea Duval's People's Republican Army and Party) and Prince Sihanouk's National United Front, continue to oppose the Heng Samrin regime and seek the withdrawal of the Vietnamese. However, in the meantime Heng Samrin has initiated purges against the coalition factions, arresting hundreds. Although the Vietnamese are being urged to leave, they've installed between 100,000 and 400,000 Vietnamese settlers in eastern Cambodia. To make matters worse, they've pursued Cambodian resistance forces into Thailand where for the first time they've engaged Thai forces in combat, indicating once again that Vietnam is intent on conquering all of Southeast Asia, as was feared by the Americans during their war with Vietnam.*

"*So, now, Mick and Bill, the world is siding with Cambodia's coalition resistance forces, which includes the Khmer Rouge, making it highly unlikely that they would be tried along with Pol Pot for war crimes in the near future. The world views them as the lesser of two evils compared to Vietnamese aggression.*"

Having been a teacher of English literature, Ing waxed poetic in closing.

"From the bottom of my heart, I thank you both for what you have tried to do on behalf of the people of Cambodia. Someday we will be free again, and prosperous when the pall of death from the Pol Pot years is swept away by the Monsoon winds and cleansed by the rain of life renewed.

Sincerely,
Ing Pech

Chapter 45

As Kathy's pregnancy progressed, it became more and more difficult for her to climb the ladder to the loft, so, because it being sweet September, she took to sleeping outside in the hammock with Mick.

"It's good for the baby to be swinging, like a cradle rocking in the boughs," she said referring to the lullaby *Rockabye Baby.*

"Yeah, and remember, when the bough breaks the cradle will fall," Mick said.

"If it does, it's your ass, Mick, for not securing the hammock well enough."

"Don't worry, Love, it was secure enough to conceive the baby in, remember?"

"Yes, it was a warm, early spring night. Your first anniversary of being sober. It's going on two years now, Mick. Do you ever get the urge?"

"In Springfield I did, so I drank a non-alcoholic beer. It tasted good, but I didn't get that addictive buzz. That's what's addictive about drinking. It sure as hell isn't the hangover, and after the first beer they all taste like horse piss anyway. Those rum and Cokes tasted pretty good, though, I must admit."

"Oh, let's not talk about drinking," Kathy said. "It's too dangerous to think about it. We call it 'stinking thinking' at AA. Remember? Let's talk about what we're going to name the baby."

"I've got an idea if it's a girl, but it might make you jealous," Mick said.

"What is it?" Kathy asked.

"Lovea."

"Why would that make me jealous? You said there was never anything between you two besides friendship."

Kathy lifted an eyebrow as if she weren't totally convinced.

"That's true," Mick said, being less than forthright.

"Well then, I think it's a lovely name."

"And if it's a boy?" Mick asked.

"I'd like to name him for my mother's maiden name, Taylor," Kathy said.

"That has a nice sound to it, Taylor Scott," Mick said.

"Taylor Stephens Scott, my maiden name."

Mick frowned.

"Well, since you took it from me when we got married, it's only fair."

The baby was born a girl. They called her Lovea and the legend lived on.

THE END

Printed in the United States
by Baker & Taylor Publisher Services